'You haven't c_____ you, David?'

'I'm older and wiser.' David's smile was relaxed but he felt disturbed. Just how much of a reputation *had* he left behind? Ok, so he'd played hard. But not that often and only as a counterbalance to the effort he put into his work. At thirty-three, David knew he was exceptionally young to have gained this surgical consultancy. He also knew that he deserved it, and he was looking forward to proving his abilities and commitment, as well as undoing this idea that he was a good-time Charlie, which might be an obstacle to professional acceptance.

Alison Roberts was born in New Zealand, and says, 'I lived in London and Washington D.C. as a child and began my working career as a primary-school teacher. A lifelong interest in medicine was fostered by my doctor and nurse parents, flatting with doctors and physiotherapists on leaving home and marriage to a house surgeon who is now a consultant cardiologist. I have also worked as a cardiology technician and research assistant. My husband's medical career took us to Glasgow for two years, which was an ideal place and time to start my writing career. I now live in Christchurch, New Zealand with my husband, daughter and various pets.'

Recent titles by the same author:

A CHANGE
OF HEART

BY
ALISON ROBERTS

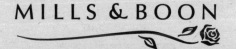

MILLS & BOON

First published in Great Britain 1999
Harlequin Mills & Boon Limited,
Eton House, 18-24 Paradise Road, Richmond, Surrey TW9 1SR

© Alison Roberts 1999

ISBN 0 263 81917 5

Set in Times Roman 10½ on 12 pt.
03-0001-48705

Printed and bound in Spain
by Litografia Rosés S.A., Barcelona

CHAPTER ONE

HEARTSTOPPING!

David James knew his heart had stopped because he was a doctor and knew about such things. He also felt the distinct thump a second later which indicated that the organ in question had decided to make up for its momentary lapse. The surprising force of the thump still failed to break the mesmerising effect of the moment.

David James was a firm believer in lust at first sight but this was definitely one for the books! She had to be the most stunning woman he'd ever seen and so far he was only getting a profile. Tall, slim, shoulder-length wavy, dark blonde hair, expertly streaked with threads of silvery gold. He couldn't see her eyes but they would have to be blue… David finally became aware that the voice beside him had continued unabated. With an effort he managed to change the static-like buzz back into words.

'So we had a bit of a reshuffle. This office seemed the perfect choice, being at the surgical end of the cardiology suite.'

'I hope I haven't put anyone out.' The husky drawl was a bit of a giveaway but had certainly not been intentional. Was it wishful thinking or did his voice have the effect of causing a momentary freezing of her decisive movements? The box was almost overflowing in any case.

'Oh, no. Lisa didn't mind a bit.'

Lisa. Perfect! It went with that elegantly tailored

clothing. That fitting black skirt with the provocative little slit that went from the above-knee hem to halfway up her thigh. David rearranged his face into what he hoped was his most charming expression as the head of Christchurch Hospital's cardiothoracic surgical team launched into a formal introduction.

'Lisa, this is our new consultant surgeon, David James.' Alan Bennett's smile reminded David of a proud parent. 'David, I'd like you to meet Lisa Kennedy, senior cardiology registrar. You two will probably be seeing quite a lot of each other.'

Play nicely, children, his tone suggested. Not a problem, David's expression assured his senior colleague as the vision turned her head towards them for the first time. Her eyes weren't blue, they were brown. Dark brown. Even better!

'I'll look forward to it,' David said aloud. He felt his smile widen further than he'd intended. It felt disturbingly close to a leer. Hastily he cleared his throat. 'I seem to have been a disruptive influence, even before walking in the door. I do apologise, Lisa. I had no idea I'd be kicking anyone out of their office.'

'As Alan said, it was the obvious choice. Like everything else in the public health system, floor space is at a premium. And, as Alan also said, I don't mind a bit.'

The tone was sweet. It just didn't match the flash of annoyance in those velvety brown eyes or the defensive tilt of her chin. Lisa Kennedy minded all right. Fair enough, too. It was a very nice office. The window had a view out to the Avon River with the glorious backdrop of the botanical gardens. Where was she going now? Probably some windowless cubbyhole down behind the exercise testing laboratory. Never mind, he'd make it up to her. His smile was understanding. Sympathetic—but helpful.

'Let me give you a hand with that.'

'No, thanks, I can manage.' Lisa hurriedly added a couple of items to the top of the carton and folded her arms around its edges. David's glance took in the elegantly tapered fingers of her left hand. Not a ring in sight! He was straightening, ready to prove his helpful intentions by insisting on carrying the box, when his companion's beeper sounded.

'I'll have to go and scrub,' Alan Bennett informed them. 'I'll leave you to get settled in, David, and we'll continue our tour later. You'll find quite a few of the old crowd still around so you should feel at home pretty quickly.'

'I do already.' David smiled. 'It's good to be back.'

Alan nodded and returned the smile as he turned away. 'You were a very popular choice for the consultancy. I wonder if so many people would welcome me back if I disappeared for a few years.'

David laughed easily but he had been surprised himself by the warmth of the welcome he'd received up until now. Up until he'd stepped into this office, in fact. Decisively, he moved forward.

'Do let me take that, Lisa. It looks heavy.'

'I *said* I can manage.' Lisa took a sideways step to evade his touch on the box. The slippery journal covers on the top layer refused to support the final item added and it slid with remarkable speed to land on the floor with a thud. A large, plastic, anatomical model of a heart, it now lay in several pieces.

David swore softly but then felt the corners of his mouth lift and couldn't suppress the smile.

'I seem to have broken your heart, Lisa.'

She *could* smile. Even the fleeting glimpse of the accomplishment was enough to make something inside David tighten with a very pleasurable sensation.

'Par for the course for you, from what I've heard, Mr James. Still, I imagine it takes first prize for speed.'

What did she mean? The tone did not suggest an attack but there was an edge to it that made David's hackles rise defensively.

'I'm sure anything you've heard is grossly exaggerated, Lisa. Pure fiction. Such rumours generally are.' He stooped to pick up the pieces of the model. 'Let me see if I can repair the damage. I'm a doctor, I know about things like this.' His smile was back in place as he straightened. He would give her the benefit of the doubt and try again.

'I wouldn't worry about it.' Her tone was offhand. 'I can assure you my heart's quite indestructible.'

This time the message was clear. David's smile finally wilted under what could only be described as a chilly stare.

'I have a ward round I should have started ten minutes ago,' she informed him crisply. 'Just put anything else in that empty box and I'll come back for it later.'

David found himself staring at the chunks of moulded plastic in his hands after Lisa swept past with her carton. She was right, of course. The solid model clipped together with a series of small brass hooks and eyes. Even its stand was unscathed. Had she intended the innuendo that the genuine article was equally impervious to damage? Quite possibly, David conceded. Lisa Kennedy obviously liked to project an image that advertised strength and competence. If the packaging hadn't been quite so attractive she might even come across as intimidating. Certainly not the type of woman David James gravitated towards.

He had to admit that her indifference to their introduction rankled. Rejection was not an experience David was accustomed to, especially from women. Taking over her office might not have been the best start but was an obstacle that could easily be overcome. Even rumours concerning any past relationships—and he had to admit there *had* been a few—could be laid to rest. Unfortunately, it was more likely that Lisa Kennedy was firmly attached elsewhere even if she wasn't married and would therefore be immune to any amount of charm he could turn on. That was a far more likely explanation. Who could look like that and not have been snapped up long ago?

With a resigned sigh, David deposited his briefcase onto the desk top and flipped open the catches. Never mind, it was still great to be back. As his indrawn breath caught the lingering trace of perfume in the office David found himself smiling. She might come across as being tough but there had to be a sensual side to a woman who wore Chanel to work. The decisive head shake as he unpacked and connected his laptop computer should have been enough to clear the distracting images of the woman from his mind, but David James was vaguely delighted to find that it failed so noticeably.

He was actually grinning as he sent himself an e-mail to test his new connection. Unexpectedly, it reminded him of his fourth-form science class when that new student teacher had taken over. Miss Drummond. Blonde hair down to her waist and legs up to her armpits. Memories of words in the science textbook blurring into total irrelevance and an entire classroom of adolescent boys squirming uncomfortably at their desks widened

David's grin even further. Even he had been in danger of dropping his position at the top of the class until he'd realised that the most effective way to get Miss Drummond's attention was to excel.

It had been a valuable lesson that had served David well over the years but until now had been simply a distant memory. Had Lisa Kennedy had that much effect on his circulating levels of testosterone? Yes. He had to admit that it seemed the only explanation for the uncharacteristic sprint down memory lane.

With a determined effort David turned his thoughts back to his surroundings and left the office. He had worked too hard to get here to have his concentration undermined the instant he walked through the door. He poked his head through an adjacent doorway.

'Hello again, Sue.'

His secretary looked up from her typing. Her smile was welcoming. Very welcoming. 'Is there something I can do for you, Mr James?'

'You can call me David, for a start.' He watched the faint flush of colour stain the girl's neck as she nodded. 'I'm just off to chase up a white coat and collect my pager. Perhaps you could give me a beep in half an hour so I can test it.'

'I'll get them for you if you like,' Sue offered eagerly.

'No. Thanks anyway, Sue, but I'm rather looking forward to exploring my old stamping ground. I'll expect a beep from you, though.'

The call came precisely thirty minutes later and David smiled as he put down the phone. A reliable and helpful secretary was a definite bonus. Like a lot of the nursing staff, Sue had probably still been at high school the last time David had worked here.

The familiar faces were all amongst the senior staff and David was thoroughly enjoying their surprised and delighted reactions as he came across them. Like Jane Maddon, who had had changed her surname but looked just the same and who was now the nurse manager of the twin cardiology wards that flanked the intensive coronary care unit.

'I knew you'd come back eventually,' she informed David, having given him a hug. 'You were so determined.'

'I love Christchurch.' David nodded. 'And a few years out of the country makes you appreciate what we've got even more.'

'I kept up with the occasional bit of news. Last I heard you were in Washington, D.C.'

'That was over two years ago. I had eighteen months in Europe after that and then had some time with a transplant unit in London. I think that experience might have been what swung the decision for this consultancy in my favour.'

'There were a lot of applicants,' Jane confirmed. 'Some were a lot older than you, too. Well done, David.'

'Thanks.' David smiled modestly.

'The parties were never as good after you left,' Jane added with a wistful grin. Then she frowned. 'You haven't gone and got married or anything, have you?'

'No chance. I was hoping you'd wait for me.'

'Oh, sure!' Jane's expression was knowing. 'I'm delighted to say you're too late.' Then she laughed. 'I'd forgotten just how cute you were, mind you. All those curls and those wonderful dark blue eyes. They're going to be queuing up around here. You haven't changed a bit, have you, David?'

'I'm older and wiser.' David's smile was relaxed but he felt disturbed. Just how much of a reputation *had* he left behind? OK, so he'd played hard. But not that often and only as a counterbalance to the effort he put into his work. At thirty-three, David knew he was exceptionally young to have gained this surgical consultancy. He also knew that he deserved it, and he was looking forward to proving his abilities and commitment, as well as undoing this idea that he was a good-time Charlie, which might be an obstacle to professional acceptance.

'I'm just on my way to check out the surgical ward,' he told Jane. 'I don't start officially until tomorrow.'

'You should be impressed. It's a great set-up.' Jane Maddon switched from old friend to professional colleague without blinking. 'Post-Cardiac Surgery Intensive Care is attached to the main ICU and the ward is right beside that. Come and have a look at CCU on your way. We've just upgraded the whole monitoring system. State-of-the-art technology.'

Jane was right. The technology was impressive and David was particularly interested by the screens which gave closed-circuit-television coverage of the most acutely ill patients. The group of staff standing by the bedside of number eight was headed by an unmistakable figure. He couldn't hear what Lisa Kennedy was saying but the examination seemed to be complete. The staff were moving away, Lisa pausing to have a final word with the patient, who was still smiling as he watched his doctor leave. David's glance flicked down to the other monitors attached to bed eight.

'You've certainly got all the bases covered.' He indicated a small button. 'I suppose this gives a printout of the ECG?'

Jane nodded. 'It does it automatically when it recognises an arrhythmia.'

'His blood pressure's low.' David was staring at the screen. His eyes narrowed slightly. 'In fact, it's still dropping.'

'Is it?'

David's eyes were back on the television screen. The curtains had been pulled open again around bed eight and he could see Lisa's back as she stood near bed seven. He heard Jane's muttered curse as she moved quickly away from the control desk and he caught the change in the ECG pattern out of the corner of his eye, but it was Lisa Kennedy he was watching. How had she known to turn back to her previous patient at precisely that point? A lightning glance at the monitor confirmed that the rhythm had slipped into the uncontrolled squiggles of ventricular fibrillation that heralded a cardiac arrest and the printout of the thin rhythm strip had begun, but it was several seconds before the alarm began to sound.

By that time Lisa had pushed the cardiac-arrest button on the wall to summon the crash team, had knocked the bed end into a horizontal position and removed the patient's pillows, pushing his bedside table out of the way as another doctor replaced it with the unit's crash trolley. Jane Maddon hurriedly pulled the curtains to screen the emergency from the horrified gaze of other patients but David had a bird's-eye view thanks to the television screen.

The staff worked as a close team. David, frustrated at his own inaction, watched as conduction pads were slapped on, positioned over the apex and bottom of the patient's heart, his bedding and clothing hastily thrown aside. It was Lisa who held the defibrillator paddles and he could almost hear her command to stand clear as other staff stepped back. He cringed inwardly as the patient jerked convulsively and then his gaze moved away from the screen as the crash team arrived at a run.

Despite the seniority of the extra staff, Lisa continued to direct the resuscitation and David's eyes were riveted to the screen as he watched the CPR, intubation and further defibrillation of the patient. He found he had been holding his breath, which he released in a sigh as the spikes of a normal sinus rhythm began to drift across the screen in front of him.

'Too slow,' he muttered, surprised by the murmur of agreement behind his shoulder. He had been totally unaware that other staff members had joined him to observe the crisis. Nobody had switched off the automatic recording of the abnormal rhythms and the strip of ECG paper was now pooling around his ankles. They all watched as Lisa injected the drugs she had ordered, presumably including atropine, and there was a collective sigh of relief within the next minutes as the observers saw the evidence of the patient regaining consciousness.

'Score one for our side, I think,' a nurse pronounced as she moved away.

Score another one for Lisa Kennedy, David amended silently. He was still watching as the crash team left and Lisa and the other unit staff tidied up. He could hear the laughter and joking and recognised the sense of euphoria he knew existed between staff in the aftermath of a desperate situation. He would very much have liked to have been included but could only smile his congratulations as Lisa and her companion passed the desk on their way out.

'Well done, Lisa,' he said warmly. 'I'm most impressed.'

'Thanks.' The smile didn't quite reach those brown eyes. 'But you must be easily impressed. It's just part of the job around here.'

'I'm sure Mr Steel wouldn't agree.' David enjoyed the surprised flicker in her expression at his knowledge of the patient's name. Then he saw her glance towards the monitors and the television screen. Her expression changed as she realised how closely David had been able to observe the incident. Fascinated by her changing expression, David wondered if Lisa Kennedy had any awareness of how her face revealed her thoughts. Her body language was expressive too. Like the infinitesimal shrug that said it was of no importance that he'd been watching her. He could almost see the effort with which she made her gaze carefully neutral when she transferred it back in his direction.

'I don't think you've met our junior registrar, Mr James. This is Sean Findlay.'

'Call me David.' He held out his hand to the registrar. 'I'm not big on formality.' His gaze included Lisa but it only Sean who nodded and returned the smile. He sighed inwardly. Was establishing a friendly relationship with Lisa Kennedy always such an uphill battle or was it something about him?

Perhaps he shouldn't have accepted Jane's offer of a tour around the cardiology wards but it hadn't occurred to David that it might coincide with Dr Kennedy's round. Neither had he had any intention of staring at the woman every time she came into view. It had to be coincidence that she managed to catch his eye every time she glanced in his direction. Or could it be that she felt the same attraction and found, like him, that she seemed to have lost automatic control over her visual targets? If so, she was very good at covering it up. Her expression became increasingly exasperated and David felt it was not before time that he headed off to explore the surgical set-up.

The unfortunate timing of his exit from the ward was more than coincidence. It was sheer bad luck. The last thing he wanted was to irritate her further by disrupting her day yet again. But what could he have done? The woman coming down the corridor was the size of an elephant. The bars on her walking frame looked seriously strained and David instinctively stepped aside to remove himself from the path of what appeared to be a human steamroller. The momentum was deceptive, however, and David found himself blocking the purposeful approach of Lisa Kennedy.

'Excuse me.'

There was nowhere to go. Jane was behind him. Lisa in front. The mountain of flesh on his left had rolled to a standstill and was breathing with alarming difficulty.

'Use your puffer, Mrs Judd,' Lisa ordered calmly. 'Have you got it with you?'

The incongruously small head nodded slowly. Sausage-like fingers inched along the bar towards a fold in a baby pink candlewick dressing-gown that looked like a bedspread. David's lips twitched. Hell, it probably needed to be a bedspread. He wanted to catch Lisa's eye to see if she was sharing any amusement in the situation but Lisa was looking over his shoulder at Jane.

'Do you have any idea where Mr Benson is?'

'Having an echo, I think.'

Mrs Judd was having difficulty locating her pocket. She tilted towards David who stepped forward involuntarily. Lisa was forced to step backwards. She looked annoyed.

'And Mrs Chisholm?'

'She was on the list for a nuclear scan but she might still be in the shower.'

Mrs Judd had found her inhaler. It seemed to be an effort for her to raise it to her lips. David heard her gasp and had a horrifying vision of trying to resuscitate Mrs Judd here in the corridor. He drew in a deep breath and was again aware of the evocative scent of Chanel. But Lisa Kennedy was looking anything but sensuous.

'It would be nice—just occasionally—if I could find my patients in their beds when I wanted to do a ward round.'

Jane laughed. 'I'll see what I can do, Lisa.'

Mrs Judd was moving again and David found himself deserted. He watched as Lisa disappeared into the ward office with Jane, before moving off himself with a small shrug. Why did he have the feeling that he was a major contributor in what was shaping up to be a bad day for Lisa Kennedy? And why did his thoughts keep returning to the senior registrar even hours later when he had finished his tour of the respiratory wards and lunched with their senior staff.

It had to be the novelty of an attractive woman apparently disliking him on sight that had sparked this preoccupation. It wouldn't take long to readjust to a professional standpoint and then they'd probably get on just fine. She was obviously good at what she did and she would soon recognise that he was also more than competent. He would gain her respect at least. And after that? a small voice whispered. David ignored the question. After that, who knew what might happen? Things had a habit of sorting themselves out. It was really only a matter of time.

And time could often pass more quickly with a little

push. David's attention was caught by the display outside the hospital's gift shop but he hadn't expected to find Lisa in residence when he managed to track down her new office. He had intended to simply leave the single red rose along with the other items in the small box he carried. With dismay he now realised that the gesture might not have been such an inspiration after all.

'I felt bad about the office,' he explained. The rose now seemed totally inappropriate but he handed it over anyway. Her expression was unreadable but maybe there was just a trace of amusement there.

'Thanks.' She tilted the rose towards the box he carried. 'I see you've fixed my heart as well.'

'My pleasure. It's what I was trained for after all.'

The reward of a smile was encouraging but David was uncomfortably aware of the reverberation of a treadmill gaining speed next door. When Sean Findlay entered the office it also felt distinctly crowded. The young registrar dumped a pile of case notes onto the second desk and vanished with a cheerful grin. The sound of the treadmill increased. David glanced out of the small window and found he could see directly into a side room of one of the cardiology wards. Mrs Judd was standing at the window. Divested of her candlewick bedspread, she was now wearing an unfortunately diaphanous nightgown. Lisa had followed her gaze.

'Just as well you weren't given this office,' she commented lightly. 'It wouldn't do to provide a surgeon with such blatant distractions.'

Something about her inflection made David's gaze transfer swiftly. 'You've got something against surgeons?'

'Nothing personal.' Lisa's smile looked mechanical.

'I'm sure you get a lot of job satisfaction.' She toyed with the rose she was still holding.

David leaned his back against the windowframe. So this was what the attitude was all about. He smiled encouragingly. 'What's so wrong with being a surgeon?'

'Oh, there's nothing *wrong*. Quite the opposite.' Lisa's eyebrows moved up expressively. 'A surgeon is the best thing to be. Ask any patient. Wait for that awed gaze when they know they're going to be referred. They're going to see the real thing.' Her chuckle was genuine enough. 'God holding a knife. A chance of a *real* cure.'

David held onto his smile with increasing difficulty. 'OK, so it's a bit more glamourous. That's not my fault.'

'More glamourous, more important, more skilled and more highly paid. A hell of a lot more highly paid.'

'Ah! Now we get down to it.' David's smile was forgotten. 'You're jealous!' David felt a flash of annoyance at her belligerent attitude and his control slipped significantly. 'So what stopped you becoming a surgeon, then? Course too tough?'

'Typical!' It was a wonder the rose didn't wilt under the heat suddenly generated around it. 'You're not good enough to be a cardiac surgeon so you take the easy route and become a cardiologist. Exactly the attitude from most surgeons and more than most of the general public. What you—and they—fail to appreciate is that you couldn't function without us.'

'Really?' David's anger had been overridden by a very different emotion. He had never been tempted to try the line that a woman looked beautiful when she was angry but, then, he wasn't in the habit of making women angry. Passionately angry, judging by the play of expression before him now. The rose was tossed aside.

'Really.' It was a snap like a steel trap. 'Who diagnoses these patients? Keeps them alive and makes the decision about whether surgery is even necessary?'

David couldn't take his eyes off her. Her guard had really slipped now. He had never seen a face quite so alive. 'I think we might have a little input into that one,' he suggested evenly. Lisa ignored him.

'Who continues the care after the surgery? They're *our* patients from go to whoa. Sure, we might need the technical assistance with a bit of replumbing in the interim but that's as far as it goes. We create your workload and we pick up the pieces afterwards. And *we* carry the can for any less than successful interventions. Envious! Listen, I know who the *real* doctors are.'

The end of the tirade coincided with the abrupt termination of the neighbouring exercise test. The silence was startling. David was still staring at Lisa. He had been watching her mouth with fascination, the soft, mobile lips now set into an uncompromising line. He met her eyes, disappointed to find that the fire had been extinguished. David raised an eyebrow eloquently but said nothing. The blush he saw appearing was unexpected.

'Sorry.' She looked away and her voice dropped to a mutter. 'I shouldn't take it out on you.'

'Take what out?' David's curiosity was aroused. Perhaps there was more going on than an irrational professional intolerance.

'It doesn't matter.'

'It seems to matter quite a lot.' David tilted his head thoughtfully. 'If I'm stepping into some political minefield, I'd prefer to get some idea of whose toes I should avoid treading on. Apart from those I've irreparably damaged already.'

'Oh ? Like whose?'

'Yours. You weren't exactly happy at being evicted from your office—at least not by a *surgeon*.'

'I don't give a damn about the office. I knew it was only a temporary luxury. It wasn't that I was…' She shook her head and then pushed a stray curl back from her face. 'Never mind. Don't concern yourself about *my* toes, David. They're indestructible.' The smile was apologetic, embarrassed even, and David was happy to return it despite the attack to which his specialty had been subjected.

'Like your heart, yes?'

'You got it.' Lisa nodded, reaching for the phone as her beeper sounded. The silence was brief. 'What's the blood pressure now? OK, stop the TPA infusion. I'm on my way.'

She was gone. David moved slowly as he followed her example. Without her physical presence he found himself thinking more about exactly what she'd said. So, he was a glorified plumber, was he? Nothing personal, though. Strangely enough, the attack hadn't felt personal at the time, but David found a new wariness nibble at the edge of his confidence. If that was the general attitude of the whole cardiology department then the obstacle to gaining respect might be a much bigger hurdle than simply exorcising any rumours about his past.

Thank goodness for a friendly face. It was late that afternoon that David encountered a welcome he'd been waiting for. It came at the end of what now seemed like a very long day.

'Mike! Where the hell have you been hiding?'

'Cath lab all morning. Then we had an emergency angioplasty this afternoon. Some of us have to earn a living, mate.'

David shook his head, confident that Lisa Kennedy's opinion of surgeons was not being reinforced from this quarter. 'It's good to see you, mate. You've been the world's worst correspondent.'

Michael Foster grasped the outstretched hand and then slapped David on the shoulder. 'Look who's talking! We must have about five years to catch up on. God, it's good to see you, Dave.'

'Likewise. Got time for a coffee?'

'I'll make time. What's the point in being a consultant if you can't manage that?'

'I thought you'd be head of the cardiology department by now.'

'Give me time. I've had a rough couple of years.'

'Oh?' David's face was concerned as he followed his friend into the small staffroom. 'What's happened, Mike?'

'Anne and I split up six months ago. Things were pretty difficult for a long time before that.' Mike spooned coffee into the mugs but glanced up to catch David's expression. He laughed ruefully. 'You were right all along, mate. Marriage is the quickest way to ruin a good relationship.' He handed David a steaming mug. 'I should have listened to that lecture you gave me. I just wish you hadn't waited until my stag night.'

David smiled but was disturbed by the shadows in Mike's eyes. He tried to lighten the atmosphere. 'You should have listened,' he said sternly. 'Like I always said, ''Why buy a book when you've got a whole library to choose from?'''

The incredulous snort from behind David made his head turn sharply. In his concern for Mike he had managed to walk right past the figure curled into the armchair beside the door. Mike followed his glance.

'Have you met my registrar, Dave? This is Lisa Kennedy.'

'We've met.' David winked at Lisa. 'In fact, I've already broken her heart.'

Mike laughed. 'That was quick even for you, mate. But I don't believe a word of it. Lisa's the one that leaves the trail of broken hearts around here. The job description for that vacancy is a bit hard to measure up to, isn't it, Lisa?'

'Oh, *please*!' Lisa uncurled her long legs from the depths of the armchair and reached for her shoes. 'I'm sure David James isn't remotely interested in my love life, Mike.'

'Oh, I wouldn't say that,' David murmured. He watched appreciatively as Lisa eased on her narrow, heeled black shoes. Very elegant footwear, he concluded. And a perfect match for the rest of her outfit.

'Well, I'm not remotely interested in sharing it.' Lisa stood up gracefully. With her heeled shoes she was only an inch or two shorter than David's height of six feet.

Mike laughed. 'That's the problem, isn't it? You'd better watch out, though. You'll probably be well up on David's required reading list.'

Lisa deposited her mug into the sink, turned and met David's eyes with a direct stare.

'My collection doesn't include paperbacks, sorry. Or over-popular fiction. I prefer something with a bit more quality…and durability.'

Mike's exaggerated indrawn breath feigned fear at Lisa's attack beautifully. Much to David's relief, it was enough to break the hold that Lisa's eye contact was having. Her short chuckle was dismissive. 'See you later, Mike. Some of us have work to do.'

David wasn't included in the farewell. Something flicked off at the dismissal and David was acutely aware of an emotional U-turn. OK, he'd been attracted but now he'd come to his senses. He'd been wrong in his assumption that the woman was attached and now he could see why. With blinding clarity. She was rude, snooty and totally unapproachable. And as for her attitude towards surgeons! Well, David James knew where he wasn't welcome and he certainly wasn't going to waste any more time trying. Lisa Kennedy wasn't going to be on any list as far as he was concerned.

Mike hadn't failed to notice the line of David's intense stare.

'Gorgeous, isn't she?'

'Mmm.' David's tone was carefully noncommittal. 'Shame about the personality.'

CHAPTER TWO

PERHAPS it wasn't so great to be back after all.

Feeling out of sorts was such an infrequent experience that David was seriously disturbed. Lack of sleep hadn't helped. Had it been a medical emergency that had kept him awake most of the night he wouldn't have thought twice about it. In fact, the adrenaline would still be running and he'd be in top form for at least another twelve hours. It was his accommodation that was problematic. The temporary arrangement for the room in the staff quarters had seemed perfect, but the walls were thin and the young medic next door had clearly scored in a big way with a woman who seemed to find the whole business excruciatingly funny. A pneumatic drill would have been much less disruptive than her giggles. Even when he'd finally managed to fall asleep the experience had been less than restful.

'It was a nightmare,' he related solemnly to Mike Foster. 'Crushing chest pain, electrodes plastered all over me and Lisa Kennedy standing at the end of the bed... Smiling.' He punctuated his tale with a woeful groan.

Mike grinned. 'Lisa's OK. Don't judge her on the basis of one bad day.' He pointed to a fire-stop door coming up on their right. 'Let's take a short cut.' Mike led the way up the stairs. 'If anybody's kept me sane over the last year it's been Lisa.' He shot his companion a quizzical glance. 'In fact, she's a lot like you.'

'What a ghastly thought!'

'She works bloody hard, plays just as hard, great sense of humour...' Mike was sounding breathless. 'And a body to die for.'

'I plan to keep living,' David muttered.

'You'd be perfect for each other.'

'I doubt it. She thinks I'm a glorified plumber. A knife-wielding technician with a God complex. Surgeons suck.'

'Ah! Well, there's a bit of a history there.'

'Oh, yeah?' Despite himself David felt curious. By tacit agreement the two men paused at the top of the stairs, screened from the corridor by another set of fire-stop doors. 'Perhaps you'd better fill me in.'

'Have you met Lewis Tanner yet?'

David shook his head. The hospital's third cardiothoracic surgeon had not put in an appearance during his tour of introduction yesterday.

'Lewis arrived about eighteen months ago—about the same time Lisa started here. ''Sex on wheels'', as one nurse was heard to report. Wealthy, confident, charming and...single.'

'And Dr Kennedy fell for him.' David nodded, feeling somehow disappointed.

'Not exactly. He fell for Lisa—in a big way. She did go out with him a few times.'

'And?'

Mike glanced around them and lowered his voice. 'Lewis presented her with an engagement ring. A rock that could have given her carpal tunnel syndrome if she'd worn it for any length of time.'

'A generous man.'

'Mmm.' Mike bit back a smile. 'Unfortunately he was overheard by a secretary telling your predecessor that he had no intention of marrying Lisa. The engage-

ment seemed to be the price he'd have to pay to get her
into the sack, so he was happy to fork out and with a
bit of luck he might even get the ring back later.' Mike
cleared his throat expressively. 'Word got around, you
know?'

'I know.' David smiled wryly. He looked at Mike
curiously. 'So Lisa knew what was going on, then? I
take it she didn't accept?'

'Oh, she accepted it. She returned it a day or two
later. Lewis was not impressed.'

David said nothing. He had a feeling there was more
to the story. Sure enough, Mike laughed quietly but
gleefully as he gave another quick glance over his
shoulder.

'Lisa had the ring valued. She put it in a clear plastic
envelope with the formal valuation. She also put in an
address of a local house of pleasure with a suggested
list of services—all couched in the most tasteful euphe-
misms—that added up to the exact worth of the ring.
Then she posted it in the internal mail system.'

David whistled silently. Half the hospital had probably seen it before it arrived at its destination. And the
other half would have heard about it.

'Photocopies of the list still surface occasionally,'
Mike added wonderingly. 'It was a major form of entertainment for months, trying to guess what some of
those services might actually be. Even Lewis came to
see the funny side—or pretended he did. I suspect it
bumped up his estimation of Lisa Kennedy no end but
he had no show after that.'

'I'll bet.' David shook his head. 'No wonder she's
not too keen on surgeons.'

'Don't take it personally.'

'Funny, that's what she said.'

'She goes out with Alan Bennett now.'

'*What?*' David was appalled. 'He's old enough to be her father.'

'It's a convenient arrangement. They accompany each other to medical functions. Lisa's great company.'

'So it would seem.' David's tone was ironic. 'Is there anyone she doesn't go out with?'

Mike laughed again. 'Yeah—Lewis Tanner.'

'Can't wait to meet the guy.'

'You don't have to wait,' Mike promised. He pushed the door open. 'Let's go and see if he's putting in an appearance at this meeting for once.'

Lewis Tanner would be in his early forties, David guessed. He was charming, sure enough. His welcome for David and apologies for missing his visit the day before were quite sincere. David eyed dispassionately the tall, impeccably dressed figure, the smooth, glossy black hair, the blue eyes and the automatic smile. David had more than a passing interest in keeping up his own appearance but Lewis Tanner made him feel distinctly scruffy. Perhaps it was the silk handkerchief or the miniature carnation in his buttonhole. Or maybe it was the unnaturally high sheen on his black shoes. Instinctively, he disliked the man and he spent the first ten minutes of the meeting trying to fathom out why.

The meeting was a regular weekly occurrence. Cardiology staff presented their referrals for surgery and decisions were made on priorities and theatre lists. The cardiothoracic team had a similar meeting later in the week with the respiratory department. David was only half listening to Lisa as she went through the scoring system on the sixty-two-year old woman being referred.

'Severe triple vessel coronary artery disease,' Lisa stated. 'Left main stem was normal but there is a seventy to eighty per cent stenosis on the left anterior descending. Dominant right coronary artery with an eighty per cent lesion in its mid-conduit portion and further fifty per cent lesion prior to the origin of the posterior descending artery.'

David watched Lewis Tanner who was watching Lisa. There was no hint of any personal animosity or long-held grudges. It was interesting to note that Lisa could hold a professional relationship with someone who had failed so stunningly to make it on a personal basis. There was hope for David yet. Lewis was nodding occasionally in agreement and his expression suggested that he was impressed at Lisa's presentation. From the angle David was sitting at he could follow the line of Lewis's gaze quite accurately, however.

Lisa had crossed her legs and David had to admit that the glimpse of thigh offered by the split skirt was arresting. When Lisa paused momentarily in her summary he glanced up and was startled to find her eyes fixed on him in a baleful glare. She looked away as soon as David caught her eye and continued her presentation, but he could have sworn her lip curled fractionally. It was only then that he realised what had caused her disgust. His tie felt suddenly over-tight. He adjusted the knot with a casual movement but his lips were pressed firmly together. Damn the woman! Now she assumed he had been sitting there thinking of nothing but her legs!

'Class one angina with ongoing pain at rest,' Lisa finished up. 'The echo shows a well-preserved left ventricular function with an ejection fraction of eighty per cent. We recommend urgent revascularisation.'

'Of course,' Lewis murmured. 'Let's get her on the list for this week.'

That was it. David forgot about Lisa—her legs, her attitude problem and even her scary ability to publicly humiliate surgeons. He found himself nodding but his agreement had nothing to do with the patient. He realised why he didn't like Lewis Tanner. The man was assuming a controlling influence in the group even though the heads of both departments were sitting nearby. He oozed confidence in his own opinion and reeked of assumed power.

David's glance shifted to Alan Bennett. The older surgeon's face was impassive as he nodded agreement but David could sense the undercurrent. He swore silently. What kind of interpersonal warfare had he stepped into? He resolved to keep silent until he got a better feel for what was going on.

He didn't have long to wait. Mike Foster launched into a polite but clearly personal criticism of Lewis Tanner.

'We don't seem to have resolved the communication difficulties between departments, Lewis. The Monday morning elective angioplasty slot is required to have surgical back-up for any emergency. You were covering this slot yesterday.'

Lewis raised his hands, palms upward, the diamond on his signet ring catching the light. 'I know, I must apologise again. It was—'

Mike interrupted him. 'It was a potential disaster. We had our patient on the table, sedated and finally psyched up for what she viewed as a major procedure. We were unable to contact you to confirm your availability.'

'That's because I wasn't available.'

'Precisely. Owing to the lack of communication, the only indication we received was the message that your cellphone was switched off.'

'I had an emergency at Greenpark. As you know.' Lewis Tanner's tone suggested that the explanation should not have needed repeating. David's brow creased thoughtfully. Greenpark was a private hospital. He had declined his own offer of operating privileges there.

'Our patient was highly stressed by the delay and eventual cancellation of her procedure. She went on to have an acute myocardial infarction and required emergency angioplasty yesterday afternoon. For which, fortunately, surgical back-up is not mandatory.'

Lewis's shrug was barely noticeable. 'She got her procedure done, then, didn't she?' He shot back a cuff to expose a discreet gleam of gold. 'I'm running out of time here. Is that it for today? Looks like we've got a full case load for the week.'

'No, that's not it for today,' Lisa snapped.

David rather enjoyed the look of irritation on Lewis Tanner's face but it was gone as quickly as it had come.

'I would like further discussion regarding the case of Desmond Knight. He was readmitted yesterday with intractable angina. In the last four weeks he has spent eighteen days in the coronary care unit. His need for surgery has become progressively more urgent.'

This time the shrug was pronounced. 'I reviewed the man last week. He's not a good risk. He's hypertensive, hyperlipidaemic and overweight. Above all, he's still smoking. As I told him, he has to be prepared to take some responsibility for the outcome of his surgery. I'm not prepared to operate until I have concrete evidence that he's given up smoking and is making an attempt to lose weight.'

'His level of angina precludes any form of exercise.' Lisa was clearly angry. 'He had cut down to one cigarette a day. The stress of receiving your letter suggesting that surgery would not be available was enough to push him back into it. He's forty-three years old with four children to support. He hasn't been able to work for six months. I'm quite confident that a chance to live a normal life will be more than enough incentive for him to make the appropriate lifestyle changes post-surgery.'

'It hasn't been enough of an incentive so far.'

David's resolve to stay silent evaporated. 'Is this a departmental policy?' he enquired.

'No, it's not.' Alan Bennett broke the tense silence. 'Lewis's principles are well known but not necessarily shared to the same degree. Desmond Knight was referred initially to Lewis but I think a change of consultant at this point might be advisable.'

'I've got a theatre slot tomorrow morning,' David announced. 'Has that been filled?'

'No.' Alan Bennett smiled. 'We planned to ease you in gradually.'

'I'm more than happy to start operating immediately,' David offered. He smiled at Lewis Tanner. 'As long as you don't object to me poaching one of your patients?'

'Not at all, old chap.' Lewis smiled back. 'Are you sure you want to? Operating on no-hopers like Mr Knight will play merry hell with your statistics.'

'I'll take the risk.' David felt as if his smile was glued on. The eye contact with his colleague was challenging. He definitely did not like this man. No wonder Lisa Kennedy was prepared to loathe cardiac surgeons on sight—particularly when they made it obvious they found her attractive. The thought made him shift his glance. The expression on both Lisa's and Mike's faces was enough reward for any risk he might be taking, politically or otherwise. If there was a line drawn in the sand here it seemed that David had unintentionally chosen which side to stand on. He was surprised at how good it felt.

'Did you hear the one about the cardiac surgeon who told his patient that he had some good news and some bad news?'

'Probably.' David grinned. 'I reckon I've heard them all by now.' Desmond Knight was a bit of a character and they had established a quick rapport during the introductory interview David had just concluded. 'Is the good news that you have twenty-four hours to live and the bad news that I should have told you yesterday?'

'No.' Desmond Knight chuckled. 'The bad news is that he's only got a week to live.'

'And the good news?'

'Well, the surgeon points to a nurse who's really...'

'Stunningly gorgeous?'

Desmond nodded enthusiastically. 'And he said, "You see that great-looking nurse over there?" The patient looks and then he nods eagerly and looks back at the surgeon kind of hopefully and the surgeon says, "Well, the good news it that I'm taking her out on Saturday night."'

David laughed with genuine amusement. He even looked in the direction Desmond had been pointing, but there was no nurse, stunningly gorgeous or otherwise. There was, however, an impressive expanse of pink candlewick—a back view of Mrs Judd, her walking frame parked in the doorway as she stopped to catch her breath. David caught Desmond Knight's eye.

'Rather you than me,' Desmond murmured.

The pink tidal wave receded, replaced almost instantly by the slim figure of Lisa. The contrast was astonishing and Desmond's face brightened considerably.

'Hi, Doc.'

'Hi, Des. I see you've met our new surgeon.'

'He tells me I'll never play the violin again.'

'You couldn't play it before.' Lisa's smile was only for her patient but David could sense its warmth and felt oddly excluded.

'I've just been explaining the surgery to Desmond here. We're scheduled for 8 a.m. tomorrow.'

Lisa nodded. 'I wondered if you had the time now to review everything. I've got all the notes and I've set up the cardiac catheter film in the viewing room if you want to see it.'

'Of course. I was about to call you.' David turned back to Desmond. 'Try and have a good rest and I'll see you in the morning.' He leaned forward conspiratorially. 'I'd better check out the home movie you had done in the cath lab. I wouldn't want to miss a bit of plumbing that needs attention.'

'Make sure you do the bolts up nice and tight. That's what bothers me.'

David could see the fear beneath the levity. He reached out and gripped Desmond's hand briefly. 'No worries, mate. I'll get you running on full bore *and* leakproof.'

The faint pink flush he could see on the back of Lisa's neck indicated that she had not appreciated the interchange as much as Desmond Knight, but David hadn't been able to resist rubbing her nose in it just a little. He would never admit to the extent that her attack had nettled him yesterday, but between that and the paroxysms of mirth from the neighbouring bedroom last night David had been sorely tempted to pack his bags and return to a more congenial hemisphere.

'What time did Desmond come in yesterday?'

Lisa was flicking a series of switches, dimming the lights in the angiography viewing room. 'About two o'clock.' She moved swiftly towards the projector. 'Why?'

'Just curious.' David took a seat, leaning back and resting his chin on one hand. The admission must have been just before he'd turned up in her office with her remaining belongings and that stupid rose. So that was what she'd been taking out on him—her frustration at being unable to provide the treatment her patient needed so desperately. Understandable. Commendable, even. But it didn't excuse her earlier rudeness or that cutting remark about library books. Lewis Tanner may well have soured her opinion of newcomers but it was still inexcusable to act on it so blatantly.

'You've got his hypertension under good control,' he commented, picking up the case notes. 'And coronary perfusion's not looking too bad.'

'Surprisingly,' Lisa agreed. She started the projector. 'We got these shots this morning.'

They both watched the screen—the shadowy background of the heart pumping, the outline of the main arteries and their filigree of branches darkening clearly as each dose of dye was injected.

David grunted. 'Not pretty.'

'No,' Lisa agreed quietly. 'It's not.'

They went through the film twice. David held the catheterisation report in his hand the second time, checking the diagram that documented which arteries were damaged and to what extent. 'We're looking at a quadruple graft here,' he murmured. 'Should keep me out of mischief for the morning.'

'Would you mind if I stood in for a while? If I get the chance, that is.'

'Not at all.' David deliberately gave his tone a professional detachment. Scrutiny was only to be expected as a newcomer, and David had never suffered from nerves due to an audience. This time yesterday his pulse rate would have jumped at the thought of being observed by Lisa but he was delighted to find himself unmoved today. Sure, the woman was physically attractive but his initial reaction had been ridiculous. She was a colleague. One who had advertised her ability to be antagonistic and would therefore need to be treated cautiously. The idea that she might be anything other than a colleague had fortunately vanished completely. He was no longer remotely interested despite Mike Foster's advocacy of her virtues and suitability. That teenage-like surge of testosterone had been nothing more than part of the excitement of starting a new job and the pleasure of renewing old friendships. The novelty had worn off amazingly fast.

The theatre team was fantastic. David was delighted to find that the anaesthetist was Gerry Greene, a contemporary and one of the old party crowd. Now married with three children, he was still keen to arrange a get-together. The nursing staff were welcoming and the selection of CDs for some relaxing background music was surprisingly good. David's choice of Dan Fogelberg was met with general approval. By the time Alan Bennett slipped in to observe, David had opened the chest, separated the sternum, retracted the ribcage and was carefully opening the membranous sac of the pericardium which enclosed Desmond Knight's heart. His registrar was doing a very competent job of harvesting the leg veins required for the grafts.

'I'm about to cannulate for bypass with aortic arterial and venous RAIVC lines,' David informed Alan.

The transfer to bypass on the heart-lung machine was smooth, and by the time David applied the cross-clamp and stopped the heart by injecting the cardioplegic solution he was thoroughly enjoying himself. David loved surgery. Politics were non-existent. The goal was defined, everybody was working on the same side and he had the skills to lead them and deal with any complications. It was a dramatic occupation. David had often thought 'theatre' was a very appropriate name for the room. It was also often highly stressful, especially when unforseen difficulties presented themselves, but David thrived on the pressure.

'7.0 Prolene, thanks.' David handled the floppy section of empty vein gently as he sutured one end of it carefully into place. 'OK. Let's check the run-off.' The adjustment of the clamp allowed blood volume to move through the graft and David nodded with satisfaction, before turning his attention to attaching the other end of the graft to the wall of the aorta.

He stood back and stretched some time later but the break in the long procedure was brief. 'Let's move on to the anterior descending, folks. We're doing well.'

Lisa did not appear in Theatre until the last graft was being attached to the aorta. It would have been easy to miss her arrival, due to the number and activity of the theatre staff, but something made David glance up. The brown eyes were magnified by being the only exposed part of her face. Even by themselves they were remarkably expressive. David dismissed the faint jolt the rec-

ognition gave him but acknowledged Lisa's presence
with a slight nod.

'Let's get this cross-clamp off and check out the
plumbing,' he suggested, his smile hidden by his mask.
David knew quite well that he'd done an excellent job.
Even Lisa should be impressed. Alan and the theatre
staff certainly were. Desmond Knight was weaned from
bypass uneventfully and his heart restarted spontane-
ously.

The atmosphere in Theatre relaxed progressively as
David wired the sternum back together and closed the
chest. Gerry Greene's plans for a dinner party had been
finalised and other staff members were talking excitedly
about an upcoming cardiovascular conference in the
South Island tourist mecca of Queenstown.

'Will you be going, David?'

'I doubt I'll be eligible for conference leave for a
while.'

Alan laughed. 'I forgot to tell you—we've got you
down as one of the speakers. I don't think leave will be
a problem and it's only for a weekend.'

David grinned. Speaking at a national conference on
short notice shouldn't be any problem and could only
speed up his acceptance. It sounded great. Unconscious-
ly, he found his gaze searching for the cardiology registrar, wondering whether she would be attending the
conference. But Lisa had vanished and David merely
shrugged mentally. It was of no great importance after
all.

'*No!* You musn't do that, Donald.'

Both David and Jane Maddon turned at the sound of
the alarmed protest. The familiar pink candlewick,
wedged between the bars of the walking frame, was
quivering ominously.

David's eyes widened. 'Don't tell me that's *Mr* Judd.' He eyed the pencil-thin, late-middle-aged man with some awe.

'Sure is,' Jane whispered. 'He absolutely adores her. He comes in every day to look after her and do her washing.'

'So I see.' David was just as awed by the size of the pair of knickers Mrs Judd was pulling from her husband's hands. Her voice had quietened due to the exertion of her protest but was still quite audible.

'If you put them in the drier they'll shrink, and then what'll I do, Donald?'

David grimaced at Jane. The alternatives didn't bear thinking about.

Jane smiled. 'We have a laundry where patients and relatives can take care of their nightwear and smalls. Donald Judd uses it more than anyone.'

'Smalls?'

Jane glanced at the item of clothing Mrs Judd had now draped over the bar of her walking frame. She elbowed David as she cleared her throat. 'What can we do for you, Mr James? Are you on the hunt for new patients? I hear Mr Knight is doing very well.'

'He is, indeed. I like the set-up in the post-surgery intensive care unit. Very impressive.'

Jane was watching Donald Judd hovering anxiously near his wife as she rolled slowly back to her room. 'Mrs Judd is in need of some attention to her coronary arteries, I believe.' She eyed David with amusement. 'We just need to get her diabetes under better control and see if we can get on top of the asthma. Lisa has her scheduled for a cardiac catheter next week.'

David was backing off. 'I really only came to find Mike. Is he around at the moment?'

Jane grinned. 'I guess Mrs Judd will have to wait, then. Mike was helping Lisa with an admission a while back. Try the staffroom.'

Half expecting to find Lisa with her consultant, David was relieved to find Mike sitting alone. The feeling changed to one of concern as he saw how morosely Mike was hunched over half a cup of coffee.

'What's up?'

'Upsetting admission.' Mike shook his head sadly. 'Fourteen-year-old boy with cardiomyopathy, Stephen Taylor. He's been on the waiting list for a cardiac transplant for over six months. Went up to Auckland a couple of months ago but it all fell through. He's not looking good right now.' Mike sighed heavily. 'Stephen's a great favourite around here. He's got a brilliant attitude to life. He's particularly attached to Lisa Kennedy. She'll probably be here all night, watching him like a hawk.'

'Are you planning to hang around as well?'

'No.' Mike stood up and emptied his cold coffee down the sink. 'Lisa's more than capable of handling things and knows when to call me if she isn't.'

'Are you otherwise free?'

'Of course. Permanent state of affairs these days.'

'Good.' David was determined to cheer his friend up. 'Gerry Greene's invited us both for dinner. Probably wants to rehash unsavoury memories. Could be just what you need.'

'Could be.' Mike was looking more cheerful already. 'Sounds great. Gerry's over the other side of town. Do you want me to give you a lift?'

'No, thanks anyway. I've bought a car and this will give me the opportunity to give it a test run. I'll meet you there at seven.'

*   *   *

The car was a heap but it had been all David could afford without putting himself into serious hock. Maybe it hadn't been such a great idea, buying his parents that town house as a present to celebrate his father's retirement. Property in central Auckland didn't come cheap. Hell, it didn't even come reasonable. Then he grinned as the engine on the aging Toyota finally caught and held. Of course it had been worth it. His parents had struggled financially all their lives and it had been their sacrifice that got him through medical school. The look on their faces when he'd presented them with the keys!

He had flown home for the occasion, having had his younger sister, Melanie, and a real-estate agent make all the arrangements. The project had had the useful spin-off of keeping Melanie out of trouble for longer than usual. His parents had been pleased enough about that— they couldn't believe it when the reason for their daughter's preoccupation had been revealed. The Jameses had only ever lived in rented houses and retirement had simply been yet another financial challenge. Now they could look forward to having the time of their lives. They were both fit and healthy.

Maybe when he got back on his feet again he'd shout them a trip through Europe. His own two-month jaunt, before returning to New Zealand, had been a wonderful experience but had also been responsible for clearing the last of his savings.

David joined the still heavy stream of traffic circling Hagley Park. At the first set of traffic lights the engine on his car died suddenly. David swore softly but got it started again just as the car behind gave him a blast on its horn. He began to feel concerned about his purchase but it seemed to be running fine until he had to slow for the roundabout at the next corner. The engine cut out without so much as a cough.

David tried to restart repeatedly as the traffic banked up around him. Cars tried to edge into the other lane to pass the obstacle he had created but other motorists were having none of it. Angry shouts and blaring horns contributed to the build-up of road rage. David opened his door, having released his handbrake. He ignored the insults thrown from a car of youths beside him and began to push, one hand on the steering-wheel, the other on the roof above the door opening. Nobody offered to help.

Once rolling, the car gathered speed and David fought to control the steering while he aimed for the side of the road. A front wheel mounted the kerb and David dived for the handbrake as he saw the cyclist on the footpath. Now he was stationary but only the front half of the car was off the road. He was still causing a traffic hazard. With an apologetic grin at the alarmed cyclist David released the catch and opened the bonnet. Surely someone would be able to offer a hand with his distress so clearly advertised.

Sure enough, a car pulled up, neatly mounting the kerb to park on the footpath, well out of the way of the traffic. A shiny, low-slung, convertible MGB. Bright red. A car buff! Just what the doctor ordered.

The driver climbed out. High-heeled shoes, long, slim legs, a neatly fitting skirt with a slit up the side.

'No…' David groaned. 'It couldn't be!'

It was. Lisa Kennedy had swapped her white coat for a tailored jacket in the same fabric as her skirt. She looked as though she would have a briefcase and several cellphones on her passenger seat.

'Having problems?'

'You haven't got a cellphone on you, have you?'

'Of course.'

'Could you ring someone for me? A breakdown service?'

'Let's have a quick look first. What happened?'

David was feeling very tense. His popularity with the general public of Christchurch was rapidly plummeting. He'd heard some pretty colourful abuse in the last ten minutes and the traffic wasn't showing any signs of abating.

'The car stopped,' he said sarcastically. 'I'd think it was fairly obvious.' He glared at the elegant figure in front of him. 'I also think it would be a good idea to clear the obstruction I'm causing.' He shut his eyes briefly. 'Now.'

'Sure.' Lisa was looking amused. 'But it would probably take half an hour for a tow truck to get here. Do you really want to wait and listen to that?'

'Get a horse!' someone yelled. Lisa's mouth twitched but she controlled her expression admirably.

David gritted his teeth. 'I don't know anything about cars.'

'Hop in,' Lisa ordered. 'Turn the key and push gently on the accelerator.'

David didn't move. 'I do know how to *start* a car,' he said coldly. 'If that had worked, I wouldn't be standing here now. And, yes, it *does* have some petrol in it.'

Lisa silently stepped around him and got into his car. The engine started first try and David swore profusely under his breath. He already felt embarrassed enough by his situation. Now he was going to look a complete idiot. The engine ran for thirty seconds and then died. Lisa turned it over but it failed to start. David was perversely relieved.

Lisa moved swiftly. Opening the tiny boot of her car, she pulled out a toolbox. Removing a torch, she marched back towards him. 'Get in, turn it on and press suddenly on the accelerator,' she commanded. Her attention was on his engine as she shone the torch into its depths.

With a frustrated grunt David did as he was told. At least he was partially hidden, sitting in his car. The insults had become appreciative whistles and hoots as Lisa leaned over the bonnet. David slumped a little further down in his seat.

'Looks like it could be a problem with your fuel line.' Lisa's voice floated through the window. 'Stay there.' She collected some items from her toolbox, including a glass jar.

'Turn the key—briefly,' she called a minute later. David complied. 'And again. OK, stop!'

David stuck his head out of the window. He watched as Lisa reconnected some tubing and then emptied the jar of petrol into the gutter.

'Blocked fuel line, I think. Try her again.'

The engine caught, held, but then died. 'For God's sake,' David muttered. 'I did ask you to call a tow truck.'

'This will only take a minute,' Lisa snapped. 'I'm going to check the spark plugs.'

David sat, drumming his fingers on the steering-wheel. The minute passed. And another. He jumped out. 'I thought you were staying in the hospital overnight.' He refused to be impressed by the confident manner with which she selected the socket and wrenches.

'I am. I'm just going home to grab a change of clothes. Stevie's asleep.' Lisa shook her head. 'Look at that. Black! It hasn't even been firing. And this one's oily, see?' She held the spark plug under his nose. 'Probably a shot PCV valve. When did you have this car in for a service last?'

'I only bought it yesterday.'

Lisa's look suggested that there was one born every day. She replaced the spark plugs and David watched as she continued working rapidly. 'You need new spark plugs, your wiring's just about had it and the battery's corroded to hell. Did you even look under this bonnet when you bought this car?'

David grinned. The funny side of the situation finally struck him. A feminist plot to destroy a manhood. A role reversal to die for. 'How come you know so much about engines?' he countered.

'I like old cars.' Lisa nodded at the gleaming machine parked nearby, wiping her hands on a rag. 'I could never have afforded to keep one on the road if I hadn't learned to look after it myself. I've had this since I was a student.' She looked back at David's car. 'How much did you pay for this?'

'Two thousand dollars.'

'Take it back,' she suggested. 'It's worth about five hundred.' She glanced at her watch. 'I've got to go. Have another try.'

The engine started instantly and chugged happily. Lisa listened for a minute. 'Your timing's way off.' She shrugged. 'Sounds like it might get you home, though.' She slammed the bonnet shut. 'I'll follow you for a block or two, just in case.'

He didn't really have any choice. Somehow it was far more unnerving to have the glimpse of the whole of Lisa Kennedy's face in his rear-view mirror than it had been to have those brown eyes critically assessing his surgical technique in Theatre that morning. Then he had been the star performer. In control. David kept his eyes on the road ahead. The tables had turned again and it annoyed the hell out of him. Another glance in the mirror a minute or two later revealed the fact that he had been abandoned. He felt even more annoyed. Then he realised that he hadn't even thanked her! David groaned aloud.

He was not only a member of a specialty that couldn't be trusted and a man with a reputation for wild parties and wilder women. He was an imbecile who couldn't purchase a decent vehicle and didn't even have a real man's ability to fix it. He had accused her of rudeness and now hadn't shown any appreciation at being rescued from an embarrassing situation. What a nightmare!

Not that he was interested in Dr Kennedy any more. Not a chance. But it wasn't very nice to feel that one's ego had been reduced in size to something that wouldn't distort a matchbox. If he kept this up, how on earth was Lisa ever going to have any idea of what she was missing out on?

CHAPTER THREE

'YOU fancy her, that's the problem, mate.'

'No way!'

'It's a gender problem, then. You don't like being shown up by a female.'

'I don't like being put *down* by a female. Or a male. Or a bloody transexual, for that matter. It's a question of whether somebody's a nice person or not.'

'Lisa's a *very* nice person,' Mike stated firmly.

Gerry nodded an enthusiastic agreement. 'She rides in like a knight in shining armour and rescues you. And you sit here, complaining that she's giving you a hard time.'

Mike and Gerry both laughed. Mike leaned over and gave David a friendly shove. 'She's just casting aspersions on your manhood, that's what it is.'

Gerry nodded again. 'And if you didn't fancy her you wouldn't be so upset about it.'

'Hey, I'm not hung up on gender roles,' David protested. 'I'm sensitive—new age. I'm not the one to have to wear the pants in a relationship.'

Mike hooted. 'That'd be right. Get them off as fast as possible, eh?'

David rolled his eyes. 'Forget the manhood issue. She's cast aspersions on my career as well.'

'She was very impressed with your surgery on Desmond Knight. Told me so herself.'

'Did she?' David was momentarily distracted. Then

he shook his head. 'Not only that. She's cast aspersions on my character.'

'Difficult to do that,' Gerry said seriously.

'Yeah.' Mike grinned. 'You'd have to work hard at it—for at least ten seconds.'

'OK, OK.' David gave up. 'But you guys haven't had your personality likened to a pulp-fiction paperback. Lacking quality and durability. She's out to get me, I tell you.'

'Lucky man,' murmured Gerry.

Mike was still grinning. 'Just because you think she's after you doesn't mean you're paranoid, mate. Don't worry.'

Gerry looked thoughtful. 'Perhaps *she* fancies *you!*'

The three men all laughed, though David's mirth was less genuine. Why was the prospect of Lisa Kennedy finding him attractive so amusing anyway? He'd never really had to entertain the possibility that he might, in fact, be *unattractive*. He watched Gerry and Mike both squash their empty beer cans.

David did not like the idea of being unattractive. He especially did not like the idea of being unattractive to Lisa. A desire for revenge was a completely alien emotion for David but he toyed with the thought as he raised his own can of lager to his lips. Wouldn't it be nice if she really did fancy him and he could cut her down to size with a subtle but spectacularly effective campaign? The thought of seeing the heat of desire in those large brown eyes did something peculiar to his gut. He dismissed the whole concept with some relief as the conversation turned.

The three friends had a great evening. Even the rug-rats Gerry had accumulated weren't a problem, having been discreetly tucked up into their beds before David had arrived. It had been the explanation for his lateness which had led to a confession of the embarrassing encounter, and they returned to the topic late in the evening after Gerry's wife had excused herself and retired, and yet another six-pack of beer had appeared from the fridge.

Mike popped the tab from a fresh can some time later. 'Yeah,' he agreed, seemingly to himself. 'They're too much of a hassle all round.'

'What, cars?' David queried.

'Women.'

David grinned at Mike's morose expression. 'What's the difference, mate? Take them for a test drive. If they feel good keep them until they conk out or get too expensive. Then—'

'Trade them in?' Gerry interrupted, shaking his head. 'Just as well everyone doesn't think like you, mate. Some of us are very happy to keep the same model and develop a more meaningful relationship.'

David groaned. 'Nappies, mortgages, more nappies. School fees, chicken pox…a partner who's too tired to talk let alone anything else by the time you finally get to bed.'

'You can't build a relationship by just having a good time.' Gerry reached for another can of beer. 'They just confirm what's already there. It's the bad times that really count.'

Mike leaned towards David. 'Lisa could give you a great bad time, Dave. She could make your life hell.'

'She already is, thanks.' David grinned. 'Why don't you ask her out yourself, Mike? You're free.'

'Damned right I am.' Mike was going to regret his alcohol intake in the morning. 'We'll go out together, mate. Forget marriage and meaningful relationships. I'll settle for loads of sex.'

David shook his head. 'It's not that easy.' He sighed heavily.

'Who are you kidding? They trip over themselves to fall at your feet.' Mike echoed David's sigh. 'Must be because you're a surgeon.'

'God, don't you start. No, the problem is age. Being thirty-something isn't great. Most of the attractive women our age are either attached or soured by a bad relationship and don't want anything to do with you. Or they've got rugrats in tow. The rest are so young they seem like kids themselves. They want commitment and deeply meaningful romance. Or loads of sex and forget the rest.'

'I'm not complaining.' Mike yawned. 'Lead me to them.'

'You'll get bored,' David warned. 'You'll end up like me, happier to go to bed with a good book.'

Mike wagged his head wisely. 'A whole library of paperbacks. I'm ready for anything.'

'You're ready for bed,' David told his friend. 'I think we'll share a taxi. My car probably wouldn't start anyway.'

The three men stood looking at the car while they awaited the arrival of the taxi.

'I had a better car than this when I was in high school,' Gerry commented.

Mike laughed. 'Hell, this probably *was* your car when you were in high school.'

'It's a heap,' David agreed calmly. 'But the guy started telling me what hard times the business was having and that's why he was prepared to sell so cheaply.

Then he started talking about all the orthodontist work his daughter needed.'

Mike put his arm around David's shoulders. 'You always were a soft touch, mate. It'll get you into trouble one day.'

'It has already,' David said ruefully. 'In fact, I may never live it down.'

'If you hadn't told them where to put those operating privileges at Greenpark, it wouldn't be problem.' Gerry shook his head sadly. 'You'd be driving a Porsche in no time.'

Mike straightened his shoulders and looked suddenly sober. 'That's right, mate. You'd earn ten times what us poor public consultants get. Big drawcard for the women, too.'

David's mouth twisted in distaste. 'I expect Lewis Tanner drives a Porsche.'

'Sure does.' Mike grinned. 'Customised number plate as well. "HEART".'

David snorted. He kicked the rear tyre of his car which had deflated considerably since that morning. 'I've got better things to do. Like research. You can't do that in private.' He glanced at Mike. 'We must have a chat about the project I want to get under way. I'm keen on looking at modified surgical techniques and their effect on the risk of cerebral damage during by-pass.'

The taxi rolled up and drew to a halt. Mike reached for the door. 'It's Lisa you should talk to. She's got a project of her own on that very subject.' He grinned over his shoulder. 'I told you you had a lot in common. Maybe she can collaborate with you.'

'Maybe she can stay out of my way.' David climbed

into the car. 'I have every intention of staying well out of hers.'

It should have been relatively easy to keep a good distance away from the aggravation that Lisa seemed so good at engendering. The respiratory and cardiology wards were well separated, there were three different cardiology teams that could call David in for referrals, and communication post-surgery or outpatient follow-up was usually done by letter. So why did Dr Kennedy have such an uncanny knack of appearing in unexpected places?

He had found her visiting Desmond Knight in the post-surgical ward yet again only this morning. The patient was doing fine. The chest and leg wounds were healing well, pain was now minimal, medical observations excellent. He was using the shower and toilet independently and had managed a full circuit of the ward without assistance at seven days post-surgery. He would be discharged and sent back to Dr Kennedy for follow-up soon enough. But the woman seemed to have a mission to personally supervise the care of every patient admitted under her team no matter what department they might be sent on to. Very admirable but a bit over the top, David thought.

And why did people around her always seem to be laughing? Or at least smiling. It had the effect of making David feel left out of something. It also had the effect of making him overly conscious of Lisa's presence, even at a distance. He could recognise her laugh anywhere—a contagious, throaty gurgle. But she had never laughed in his company and David had always been aware of his own ability to lighten almost any atmosphere with a joke or two and make people laugh.

With Lisa his comments fell like lead balloons. She refused to be amused when he was around, unless it was at his expense.

Like yesterday, when he'd been sitting in CCU, reading a patient's notes, and Jane had gone past and ruffled his hair. He had felt obliged to chide her on her disrespect but Jane had merely laughed.

'Couldn't resist,' she had excused herself. 'It's so...' She'd been searching for an appropriate adjective as Lisa had walked by with a length of ECG trace in her hands. Lisa had taken a long look at David's hair.

'Hmm,' she had murmured thoughtfully. 'Did you sue the hairdresser, David—after the perm?'

Jane had laughed again. 'It's always been like that. Gorgeous, isn't it? Like a mobile pot-scourer. It's even got that metallic gleam.'

David had scowled. His corkscrew brown curls with their natural highlights were distinctive, and he knew quite well they made him appear younger and less professional than he might have done, but his one attempt at shaving them off had been disastrous. With his thin face and wide smile he had looked as though he'd suffered through a particularly gruesome course of chemotherapy. So he was stuck with the curls, but David didn't like being labeled as 'cute'. He would have preferred a suave and sophisticated image—like that which Lewis Tanner seemed to project so effortlessly. On second thoughts, maybe he didn't. Curls were cool. David smiled.

'People have been known to pay big money to get a hairstyle like this,' he informed Jane. 'I happen to be fortunate enough to have it as a natural attribute.'

'It's natural all right,' Jane grinned. 'I love it.'

'Me, too.' The echocardiograph technician, Jenny,

had joined them at the control desk. 'Are you still OK for tonight, David?'

'Can't wait.' David gave Jenny his most brilliant smile, grateful for the change of subject. 'Eight o'clock, right?'

'Here we go again.' Jane gazed heavenwards. 'Another one bites the dust.'

Lisa had found the set of notes to file the ECG strip into. She snapped them shut and moved away with Jane. 'Perhaps Jenny has some pots that need scouring,' she said clearly. Both women were laughing as they left the unit.

Perhaps he was simply overreacting to her barbs. Perhaps it was because she treated him so differently to other colleagues. She had a close friendship with Mike. Was he jealous of their easy rapport? No. Mike was a great guy. Renewing their old friendship, that had, so far, been the best aspect of his return. He was glad that his mate had good friends who had been around to help him through a difficult patch. Lisa had a similar rapport with many other staff members and the patients thought she was wonderful. Desmond Knight was smitten.

'She's the best,' he had told David on more than one occasion. 'She really cares, you know?'

Most registrars kept a personal distance from consultants or at least some degree of deference. But Lisa seemed to be welcomed as an equal. Especially by Alan Bennett. He saw his boss with Lisa now, beside the photocopying machine, as he headed back to his office after lunch. Kissing her, no less! On the cheek, admittedly, but it had prompted David to slow down so that Lisa was alone by the time he reached her.

'You seem to get on well with Alan.'

Lisa glanced up. The raised eyebrows and cool expression informed David that it was none of his business. David lowered his voice. 'How does Alan get on with Lewis Tanner?'

Lisa looked startled. 'Why do you ask?'

'I have to work with them both. I've already got the strong impression that Lewis has a rather consuming personal agenda. Not one that I find particularly attractive.'

Lisa kept her eyes averted. She carefully positioned a journal page on the glass top of the photocopier. 'Lewis Tanner is committed to his private interests. Public hospital work provides a useful extension.'

'Useful?' David was puzzled.

Lisa's glance was searching. It was long enough for David to register just what a rich shade of brown they were. Velvety. Dark. Like the chocolate on expensive after-dinner mints. A man could drown in eyes like those. David brought his attention to heel sharply. Not this man! She seemed on the point of making a decision about whether or not she could trust him. On the point of speaking, in fact, until the machine light flashed and Lisa lifted the journal to turn the page. 'Ask Mike,' she suggested. 'My opinion is a little too biased to share.'

'Why does Alan put up with him?'

'Alan's a peacemaker,' Lisa said carefully. 'And he has a foot in both camps.' She collected the sheaf of photocopied pages, before looking up at David. 'He is also an exceptionally diplomatic person. He's very good at what he does and he avoids causing offense if at all possible. Unfortunately, he will probably head back to Australia. He came here after his wife died but he misses his children and has a grandson now. I suspect he'll go as soon as a suitable position becomes available.'

'That's a shame.' David was now feeling uncomfortable. How could she make the description of someone else feel like a personal criticism of himself? Or was it simply another overreaction?

'Lewis will probably go as well,' Lisa continued evenly as she turned to leave. 'He'd much prefer to work full time in private.' She flicked David another glance, this time a little calculated. 'You might find yourself head of department before you know it.'

David stood back to let her pass. 'You're not too impressed by cardiothoracic surgeons, are you, Lisa?'

Her gaze was now a challenge. 'Should I be?'

David should have stepped a little further back to let her pass. That way she wouldn't have brushed his chest with her shoulder as she moved. That way he wouldn't have been aware of the sensation the touch generated, a sensation that seemed to make it difficult to draw breath. He forced a grin onto his face. 'That's your decision, Dr Kennedy. Maybe one day you'll change your mind.'

'Maybe.' Lisa's smile also looked as if it had taken an effort to produce. 'One day.'

Aggravating, opinionated and arrogantly superior. He should loathe the woman. So why did he have this sneaking admiration for her unshakable standpoint and the feeling that he was missing out on something important due to the force field she had erected? Especially, why did he feel the need to impress her? He only wanted a professional rapport. The same as she allowed everybody else, with the understandable exception of Lewis Tanner. He didn't want a personal involvement. God forbid! Even if she was panting for him he wouldn't touch her with a barge pole. Not even for a sweet taste of revenge.

So why should he feel any inclination to impress her, let alone a preoccupation that was threatening to become disruptive? David was on his way to answer a request for a consult on the respiratory ward. A patient didn't seem to be responding to the treatment for a pneumothorax and his consultant wondered if surgical intervention might be necessary.

David stalked through the corridors, his mind not yet on the patient he had been called to see. It came down to personal esteem, he decided. His ego had taken a distinct battering, thanks to Lisa Kennedy. Word of his embarrassing mechanical problems had leaked out. He suspected that Gerry Greene had been keeping theatre staff entertained by embellishing the story. He had the horrible suspicion that because it had been Lisa involved the comparison between himself and Lewis Tanner would be established on a personal basis. That was only a step away from being likened to his colleague professionally and that was definitely unacceptable.

Lisa was the key. If he could impress her then the link would be broken and David could restore his own pride.

A registrar introduced him to the patient, thirty-four-year-old Wayne Drummond, and David made a quick examination of his chest and the drainage system in place.

'You're right,' he told the registrar, folding his stethoscope. 'The lung's not fully inflated yet but I think it's just a matter of keeping the suction going for a bit longer. I don't think surgery's indicated.'

'Hallelujah!' his patient muttered. 'This place gives me the creeps as it is. Reminds me of my father's fate.'

'What was that?'

'Keeled over and dropped dead when he was forty,' Wayne said. 'I was just a kid.'

David glanced at the registrar who raised her eyebrows and looked worried, probably because it wasn't detailed in the patient's notes and could be an important issue. He turned back to Wayne.

'Have any other members of your family had a sudden death at an early age?'

'My uncle died when he was in his thirties. I never knew any of my grandparents. Not a great track record, is it?'

'No, it's not,' David agreed cheerfully. 'Maybe I'll check you out a bit more carefully.'

'No. Sooner I get out of here the better. I just wish I'd been a bit more careful on the stairs.'

'Can you remember exactly what happened?'

'Not really. I think I just tripped and landed on the bannister post and broke my ribs. All I remember is waking up on the floor with a bloody sore chest.'

'Waking up?' David had his hand on Wayne's carotid pulse. 'Did you hit your head?'

'No, don't think so. It's not sore.'

'Is it possible you blacked out and that was what caused the fall?'

Wayne shrugged. 'I can't remember.'

'Have you ever had any dizzy spells or blackouts?' David was unwinding his stethoscope again.

'Get a bit light-headed occasionally,' Wayne said thoughtfully. 'Jeez, Doc. I'm not going to conk out like my dad did, am I?'

'Not if I can help it.' David was silent as he listened,

the stethoscope positioned above the chest drain over Wayne's heart. 'OK, Wayne.' David straightened. 'I'm going to get you out of bed for a minute.' He unhooked the drainage bottle from the bed-frame and held it in one hand, the disc of his stethoscope still held in his other hand.

'Hang onto the bed with the arm on your good side,' David instructed the young man. 'I want to listen to your heart while you squat and then stand up.'

He nodded as Wayne complied with the manoeuvre. As he had expected, the abnormal murmur he'd detected diminished when his patient was in a squatting position and increased markedly on standing. He and the registrar helped Wayne back onto the bed as the registrar's beeper sounded.

'Sorry, I'll have to go,' she apologised.

'No worries.' David's smile was casual. 'I might keep Wayne company for a bit longer. You don't have a twelve-lead ECG machine around here, do you?'

'Sure, in the treatment room.'

It had been a long time since David had done a twelve-lead ECG himself. He was rather enjoying a return to some basic cardiology. Lisa was renowned for her care of patients not necessarily strictly within her own specialty. Perhaps two could play at that game. When he had successfully placed the electrodes on Wayne's ankles and wrists and positioned the rest in a pattern around his heart, he stood back, his finger poised over the start button. Wayne was looking apprehensive, as though he expected to be electrocuted, but he smiled when he saw David's satisfied expression. David ripped off the page of trace results.

'I'm just going to make a quick phone call,' he told Wayne. 'Be back in a minute.'

Jenny, the echocardiograph technician, seemed delighted to hear from him. 'You're in luck,' she told him. 'I've got a gap right now. Wheel him over. You can do the echo yourself if you like.'

'Great. After your tutorial last night I might just manage it. Thanks again, Jenny.'

'My pleasure. You owe me a bottle of wine, don't forget.'

'I won't,' David promised. 'We'll be there in five minutes.'

An hour later David made another phone call, this time to the operator. 'Who's the cardiology team on take today?' he queried.

'Michael Foster.'

'Great. Could you page him for me, please?'

An unfamiliar voice answered the page. 'Do you have a message for Mike?' it enquired.

David gave the details of the referral. Then he went back to check on Wayne. He was looking forward to Mike's arrival. He knew his mate would be impressed. But it was Lisa who came through the door of the respiratory ward ten minutes later. Walking to meet her, David was momentarily disappointed but rallied quickly. This was even better. At last he had the chance to impress the woman.

'Mike's caught up with a temporary pacemaker insertion. He said he'd catch up with you later and not to forget about the double date you've got tonight.' Lisa spoke as though she were communicating information on a patient's test result. 'He said he's lined up the two best-looking cath lab nurses you've ever seen.'

David groaned inwardly. 'Mike wants to hit the bachelor scene again and thinks I'm some sort of expert. I think he'll be disappointed.'

'So do I.' Lisa fiddled with the stethoscope that protruded from the pocket of her white coat. 'Not by any lack of expertise on your part, of course.' Her gaze locked with his. 'He still loves Anne, even if he denies it. Did you know they have a baby?'

'No.' David was shocked. And then he felt angry. Mike was a special friend. How come Lisa knew more about his private life than he'd been allowed to share?

'It was all part of the problem. Anne had a very difficult pregnancy and then mild postnatal depression. Mike was struggling with political hassles, thanks to our friend Lewis. It all got too much.' She sighed. 'Anyway, I hope you all enjoy your night out. What's the problem here?'

David wanted to talk more about Mike but Lisa had made it suddenly inappropriate. 'Come and meet him. Wayne Drummond, thirty-four. Came in yesterday with broken ribs and a pneumothorax. It's been slow to respond to drainage and when I was checking him I noticed a bit of a murmur.'

Lisa was nodding. They had reached the patient's bed. 'Hi, Wayne. I'm Lisa Kennedy. I'm a cardiologist and I'd like to have a listen to your heart, if that's OK?'

Wayne nodded. David stood back, listening and watching. She certainly did better than the respiratory registrar, eliciting the information about his family history within the first couple of minutes. She took a blood-pressure reading and then he watched her hand on Wayne's neck as she felt his carotid pulse. A plain gold bangle fell back against a slim wrist. He could imagine how gentle her touch was.

For a second he wondered how it would feel to have those delicate fingers touching his own skin and had to look away as he quelled an entirely unprofessional twinge of desire. Perhaps the night out with the nurses wasn't such a bad idea after all. His sex life had obviously been neglected for too long. By the time he looked back, Lisa was listening to Wayne's chest, front and back.

'I'd like to get you out of bed, Wayne, so I can check your pulse standing and squatting.'

'Not again!' Wayne groaned. 'It kind of hurts to move and Mr James has already done that one.'

Lisa looked taken aback. David suppressed his smile. He enjoyed every second as Lisa excused herself and they both moved away from the patient.

'There's a definite systolic ejection murmur,' Lisa said quickly. 'I'd pick mitral regurgitation or aortic stenosis. We'd better transfer him to Cardiology and do some more investigations.'

'Like a twelve-lead ECG?' David produced the page from his pocket. Lisa gave him a strange look, before turning her attention to the trace.

'Left bundle branch block,' she muttered. 'Still points to aortic stenosis. Q waves are pretty deep. Could be—'

'Hypertrophic obstructive cardiomyopathy?' David delivered the suggestion thoughtfully, relishing every syllable.

'Possibly. We'll need to do an echo.'

David produced the page of echo results from his other pocket. Lisa stared at the paper and then at David.

'You've already made the diagnosis and done the appropriate investigations.' Her tone became sarcastic. 'I suppose you've started treatment as well?'

'Yep.' David's grin sneaked out. 'Beta blockers. Propanolol 160 mg, four times daily.'

Lisa looked resigned. 'I suppose I deserve this.

You're trying to show me that cardiologists are redundant. Surgeons can do anything.'

'Not at all.' David could afford to be generous. He smiled placatingly. 'I just thought you might be impressed by the fact that we can be real doctors, too, sometimes.'

'OK, I'm impressed.' She didn't look impressed. She looked annoyed. 'I've just wasted half an hour, that's all.'

'I needed your authorisation to transfer him to Cardiology,' David reminded her. 'And I thought you'd prefer to make your own initial assessment. Will you follow up with a Holter monitor or catheterisation?'

'Possibly.' Lisa nodded. 'If he has a significant left ventricular outflow tract gradient we'll send him back to you for some surgery.'

'"Pass the Patient",' David grinned. 'Kind of like "Pass the Parcel" only there's less to unwrap.'

Lisa returned the grin. He had succeeded in amusing her! Not enough to make her actually laugh but it felt like a major triumph. David felt a glow of satisfaction.

'How did you get Jenny to do an echo at such short notice?'

'I have this incredible power over women.' David leaned closer. He could smell the Chanel and it suddenly seemed the most evocative perfume ever invented. 'I can get them to do anything I desire.'

Lisa edged away. Her look was exasperated but David realised that his physical proximity had affected her more than his words. She looked distinctly unsettled. He watched the faint pink flush enter her cheeks. The glow he had felt in his success at amusing her faded, replaced by a knot of tension that David failed to recognise. His lips seemed to move without any conscious direction.

'Come out to dinner with me, Lisa.'

'You have no power over me, Mr James.' Lisa took another step back. 'I'm a cardiologist, not a woman.'

It was an open invitation to allow his gaze to travel down the length of the elegant figure before him. Lisa had a dark yellow dress on today, slim-fitting and very smart. As far as David was concerned, she was *all* woman. Yet her comment seemed quite serious.

'Does being a *real* doctor mean that you can't be a *real* person as well, then?'

Lisa eyed him silently. For a second, David was sure he'd actually been allowed to step inside the force field. 'In my case, it could be true,' she said quietly.

David had to suppress the urge to reach out and touch her. To extend the moment of connection. The power of the urge was enough to rattle him badly so, instead, he just grinned. 'Thank God I'm only a surgeon, in that case.'

She didn't bother to answer that. She just walked off, shaking her head. Thank goodness. David breathed a sigh of relief. What would he have done if she'd accepted that impetuous invitation? An intimate dinner with this woman was the last thing he'd want.

Wasn't it?

CHAPTER FOUR

THIRD time lucky, David decided, stripping off his blue theatre gear.

It was the first time his Wednesday morning cardiac surgery had finished in time for him to attend the lunchtime meeting. He had particularly wanted to make this one, having seen the memo detailing today's speaker. It was a meeting open to all interested medical staff members. A rotation allowed all departments to put forward interesting cases for presentation. The purpose was to maintain a hospital-wide link, to provide information of perhaps the appearance of a new viral disease, improved diagnostic techniques or therapies. In some cases it gave an open forum for the input of suggestions to deal with a particularly troublesome case.

Lisa's presentation did not fit any of these criteria. As David eased himself through the door, to stand with others who had been too late to secure a seat in the packed lecture theatre, the lights were dimmed and an image appeared on the large screen—a young man, grinning in typical adolescent embarrassment at the attention of the camera, his hand held up to one side of his face with a triumphant thumbs-up gesture. It advertised an unusual approach. Patients were normally presented anonymously, identities protected by the use of initials and certainly no photographs.

Lisa waited for complete silence. Her voice, amplified by the microphone clipped to the lapel of her white coat, was soft but confident.

'We are all faced with a huge number of people need-
ing our medical assistance. Some we instinctively like,
some we can't stand, but we try our best to offer com-
passionate and hopefully effective therapy…without becoming too emotionally involved.' Lisa cleared her
throat delicately. 'Occasionally we are faced with a case
that makes it impossible to avoid that involvement. This
is such a case. The case of Stephen Taylor.'

David, like everyone else in attendance, felt his attention focus sharply.

'Twelve months ago, Stephen Taylor was your average thirteen-year-old boy, physically speaking. In
other respects he was very far from average. Stephen's
IQ had been estimated to be in excess of one hundred
and fifty. His ambition to become a doctor seemed an
easy goal. He was already doing university-level science subjects and taking an extracurricular course in
anatomy. Not that he was a complete academic nerd…'
Lisa waited for the ripple of laughter to subside.

'Stephen has a passion for old rock and roll, particularly the Rolling Stones, an equal passion for classic
cars and a girlfriend he has been keen on since primary
school. He has three older sisters who adore him and
parents who provide a stable and very loving family
environment.

'Twelve months ago the world was Stephen Taylor's
oyster and he was loving every minute of it. Last winter
he caught the flu.' Lisa cleared her throat again. 'A few
days off school. A bit inconvenient but not a major
hassle. Something we—and our children—have to handle with monotonous regularity. He was back to school
the next week but he couldn't quite shake off the virus.
He seemed to be tired all the time, got short of breath
with minimal exertion, had the odd palpitation and even

a few spells of dizziness...' Lisa paused briefly. 'And his shoes felt uncomfortably tight.'

A few heads were nodding amongst the audience. Lisa was looking around as she continued speaking. 'One day, during a history class, Stephen collapsed. It could very easily have been a sudden death—the type of case we hear about more frequently than we'd like to. But Stephen Taylor was still alive when the paramedic team arrived. And he was still alive when he was admitted to our care in the CCU a short time later.'

The teenager's face disappeared from the screen and the lights came up as Lisa moved to an overhead projector and flicked the switch. The silence was still absolute. The case presentation so far had been very far from typical. Nobody presented a case in such a personal manner. What was she doing? David wondered as he watched the overhead transparencies detail the results of exhaustive tests. Had the lad died? Was Lisa going to discuss the implications of becoming too emotionally involved with patients?

He registered the data—the physical examination and findings, the ECG, chest X-ray, echocardiograph and the cardiac catheterisation. The diagnosis was clear-cut. Congestive cardiomyopathy—a complication of a viral infection which had led to a dilated, poorly contracting left ventricle and progressive heart failure. There was no need to discuss the results—or the treatment. Mike and Lisa had brought the heart failure under control with an impressive drug regime and had kept the boy under close observation.

Somebody's beeper sounded and they moved past David to get through the door. He found himself taking the empty seat automatically. His attention was not diverted. It was like reading a thriller. He had to know the ending of the story and the motivation for the main character. From his perspective right now, the main character was Lisa Kennedy. Did everyone else find their eyes riveted so totally on that slim figure on the podium? Did every inflection in her voice and subtle change in her body language elicit such an acute response of their own awareness, as David was experiencing?

'Stephen Taylor went on the waiting list for a cardiac transplant six months ago,' Lisa was saying. 'He carried a pager, waiting for the call that would mean a dash four hundred and fifty miles north to Auckland. He took it to school for the classes he still managed to attend. He kept it beside his bed at night. The call came two months ago at 4 a.m. A woman involved in an MVA in Wellington was available as a donor. The size match was perfect. Even the blood group was an exact match. By 5.30 a.m. Stephen, his mother and myself were in the Medivac plane *en route* to Auckland.'

The atmosphere in the lecture theatre was tense— almost a collective holding of breath.

'Stephen was prepped for Theatre on arrival. He was scared but excited. This was it! The miracle we'd all been hoping for. The donor heart arrived by helicopter at almost the same time. The patient was ready, the surgeons were ready. The anaesthetist was on the point of starting induction when we were told there was a problem.'

The sigh was also collective. Lisa's tone hardened. 'The heart was unsuitable. Hypertrophic. The donor had been an undiagnosed hypertensive, probably for a long time. There was also evidence of coronary artery disease. Nothing could be done. Stephen and his mother were offered accommodation in Hearty Towers, the facility for transplant patients and their families from out of town, in the hope that another donor might become available. Stephen refused. He didn't want to be away from his family or friends. And he didn't want to get behind in his schoolwork.

'The heart failure is end-stage and becoming very hard to control. Stephen has had three admissions since the abortive rush to Auckland. Each one has potentially been his last. This one probably will be.' Lisa looked down in silence for a second and then raised her face, her chin up. 'You're probably all wondering what the point of my presentation is. Even if a donor became available tomorrow, Stephen is too ill to travel to Auckland. We all have tragic cases that touch us very deeply. What's so special about this one?'

Lisa looked around at her audience. David had to admire her poise. She had them all in the palm of her hand. 'The point is that we have reached a turning point in the treatment of such cases in Christchurch. Thanks to a recent appointment, we have the skills available to perform a cardiac transplant right here. I'd like to introduce Mr David James to those of you who don't already know him by past acquaintance or reputation.'

The collective chuckle was friendly but David felt himself reddening. Lisa's eyes found David with an unnerving rapidity. Had she been aware of his presence all along? 'Could you stand up, please, Mr James? I'm sure everyone would like to see who you are and welcome you to Christchurch.'

Reluctantly, David got to his feet briefly, to a wave of applause. He felt embarrassed and vaguely threatened. What did Lisa expect of him? That he could somehow wave a magic wand and provide a miracle for a case that was now going to be a focus for the entire hospital community?

Lisa was collecting her overhead transparencies. 'I know it's not always easy approaching a family regarding the question of organ donation.' She looked up again and David's head turned, with many others, to the knot of people he recognised as representing the ICU. 'I just wanted to remind people of the other side of the coin. The story of a potential recipient. The story of Stephen.' Lisa dimmed the lights, reaching an unexpected and dramatic conclusion by again projecting the boy's photograph.

There was a moment's complete silence and then a general buzz of conversation broke out. David checked his watch and was astonished to find that lunchtime was now over. Lisa's presentation had filled the entire forty five minutes. Nobody else had said a word. They had been caught spellbound by the account and left with the lasting image of a courageous youth giving a thumbs-up signal.

Working his way through the throng of people dispersing towards their various destinations, David found himself unexpectedly eye to eye with Lisa. He bowed his head slightly.

'Bravo, Lisa. You missed your vocation, I think.'

'Sorry?'

'You had your audience captivated. You could do well on stage or screen.'

'Ah!' Lisa raised her eyebrows quizzically. 'Next act perhaps—enter cardiac surgeon, stage right. The hero of the hour.'

David frowned at her sardonic inflection. She was going to get squashed by the weight of the chip on her shoulder if she wasn't careful. He'd had enough of it. 'Look here, Dr Kennedy—'

Lisa ignored his growl, her gaze elsewhere. 'Enter, stage left, John Watson. Intensive Care consultant. Hi, John! Have you met David James?'

'I have, indeed. You might like to fill me in on his past reputation, though.' John's grin at David was friendly but his expression amused. 'What gossip have I missed out on yet again?'

'Ask a nurse.' Lisa laughed. 'Any nurse!'

David fixed Lisa with a steely glare as he gave an exasperated sigh, but John's grin widened. 'You'll have to let me in on the secret. Unfortunately, it's a bit late in my case.' His grin faded rapidly. 'Seriously, now, I'm glad I've caught you. Both of you.' John Watson looked from David to Lisa. 'We've got a young woman in the unit. Serious brain injury from an accident last week. The EEG hasn't picked up and we've got a family conference this afternoon.' The consultant spread his hands. 'I don't want to raise any hopes yet—it's only a possibility and I have my doubts about her husband's reaction.'

David was watching the glow ignite in Lisa's eyes. Fat chance of not raising hopes, he thought. The woman looked like she'd just been told she'd won first prize in a lottery. He found a smile gently curving the corners of his own mouth as his anger faded. Despite the superiority complex and all the angst, someone who cared that much about a patient couldn't be all bad.

'Act two, scene three,' he suggested quietly. 'Theatre.'

Lisa let out her breath in a long sigh. 'Let's hope so.' The glance she gave David was almost beseeching and David was shocked at the jolt it gave him. Whatever she was asking of him he was prepared to give—and more. Unsettled by his reaction, David turned away.

'Let's,' he agreed calmly. He glanced back quickly. 'It may be the only chance I have to salvage my reputation, thanks to you.'

'Your reputation is entirely your own,' Lisa retorted. 'If it needs salvaging it has nothing to do with me.'

He could swear he heard her added mutter of, 'And thank God for that.' But he couldn't be sure and he was now staring at a rapidly retreating back. Lisa certainly had the knack of needling him but his own response was too quick and too exaggerated. A personality clash, he concluded unhappily. He would just have to set a mature example and show Dr Kennedy how it could be dealt with without compromising a professional relationship.

That resolve lasted all of three hours. Until he was actually face to face with Lisa again. The brown eyes were flashing fire and David knew that something had hit the fan. Judging by the way she'd burst into his office and stood glaring at him, it was something that could somehow be directly attributed to himself. A wave of weariness washed over David as he pushed himself to his feet. An advantage of at least an inch or two in height seemed a good first line of defence.

'What have I done now, Dr Kennedy?' It was easy to make his tone exasperated. He really was fed up with being a target for this bolshy woman whose passions seemed rather misplaced—and wasted.

'You operated on Mr Waugh this morning, didn't you? Douglas Waugh?'

'Yes.' David straightened his spine a little more. 'A mitral valve replacement. Quite successful, I think.'

'Mike tells me you used a femoral arterial cannulation for bypass rather than a standard ascending aortic cannulation.'

'It's an acceptable alternative. Especially when patients are undergoing repeat surgery.'

'Mr Waugh was not undergoing repeat surgery. This was his first, and possibly only, procedure under bypass.'

'Well, let's hope so.' David frowned. 'Look, what is this all about, Lisa? Have you come here just to criticise a decision I made regarding my surgical technique? If so, I'd—'

'Did you have a reason for modifying the cannulation site?' Lisa interrupted him. 'Other than adding a little variety to the procedure?'

'Yes, I did,' David snapped. '*If* it's any of your business. I'm looking at the effects, if any, of modified cannulation and clamping sites on post-bypass cerebral damage. Mr Waugh is the first patient of a series I intend to extend considerably. It's a research project I've looked into before but I've never been based anywhere long enough to make it a feasible proposition.'

'Did you get a signed consent form from the patient regarding his participation in this trial?'

'It's not a trial. At this point it's an observational study. And I don't normally obtain signed consent forms regarding a perfectly acceptable modification of a surgical technique. Mr Waugh is not even one of your patients. I fail to understand what your problem is.'

Lisa took a deep breath as she stared at David. She seemed to be making an effort to control herself. When she spoke, her tone had calmed considerably.

'I have been working for some months to get a controlled, double-blind, randomised drug trial under way. I have received drug company, departmental and ethical committee approval. Have you heard of the drug Neuroshield?'

The name rang a bell but it was quite difficult to dredge up any details. A conversational topic or a media report at some stage in his travels. Wonder drugs were always being discussed—often years before they had any chance or making an appearance in clinical practice.

'It has some action on cellular metabolism, doesn't it? Specific to cerebral cells?'

'It has the ability to slow the metabolism radically. As far as the animal studies can predict, it gives close to perfect preservation of cerebral cellular function under some remarkable challenges. Its use as a prophylactic agent to prevent cerebral damage during bypass surgery has a lot of people interested.'

David was now interested himself. He was watching Lisa intently.

'Mr Waugh was the first patient I had enrolled. I obtained an informed, signed consent form from him and completed baseline anatomical and functional assessment two days ago, including a CT scan. I administered the dose of either Neuroshield or placebo myself. This morning.'

'What time this morning?'

'Six-thirty a.m. I came in specially. The protocol is to administer the dose two hours prior to surgery.

Six-thirty a.m. Thirty minutes before David had arrived to review his patient and prepare for surgery. 'I didn't see any warning marker on Mr Waugh's chart that he was enrolled in any trial or had been administered any drugs not charted by myself.' David's tone was icy. This was serious and could have unfortunate repercussions.

Lisa flushed. 'I had the stickers in my pocket,' she admitted reluctantly. 'I put one in his notes but not on his chart. One of the nurses had taken it to record his pre-op observations.' She met David's glance. 'Don't worry. Even if it wasn't the placebo, Neuroshield has no known interactions with any other drugs. I was excited about actually beginning the trial. I went to review the CT scan and book in the follow-up in three days.' Lisa sighed angrily. 'Not that there's much point now. Modifying your surgical technique adds conflicting data that I haven't allowed for in my protocol. I'll have to start again.'

'Randomly dosing my patients with a trial medication will confuse my own data. Perhaps we'd better agree to keep our studies completely separate.'

Lisa dropped her eyes. 'In that case I'll have to abandon the trial. I wouldn't be able to get the case numbers I need.'

'Why not? I only represent thirty per cent of the surgical team.'

'Lewis doesn't wish any of his patients to be involved. In fact, he was delighted to provide the only real obstacle I have had to contend with. That only leaves Alan's patients, and it would take me years to accumulate enough for even a pilot study. Someone else will have done it well before then.'

Damn it. Her disappointment and frustration were palpable. It should feel good. Lisa was not on top of this situation. Here was an opportunity to take revenge, presented on a plate. David could provide an obstacle just as big—even bigger—than Lewis had. He could block her research interests completely. But he didn't want to. Quite the reverse.

'There is another possibility,' he found himself suggesting.

'You'll give up your observational study?' The light of hope dawned in the brown depths of her eyes.

'No.' The light went out but David held her gaze and spoke slowly. 'We could collaborate.'

Her eyes widened. The stare was intense. David wondered if anyone had ever listened to him as closely as Lisa's face advertised she was about to.

'What about a multi-factorial study design? Four factors. Medication, modified surgical technique, nothing or both.'

'It wouldn't be double-blind.'

'The medication side would be. We could randomise the surgical technique as much as possible. It would give a lot more data. And be a unique study. I doubt if anyone else trialling Neuroshield would be making life more difficult for themselves by extending the factors.'

'We'd have to start again. Talk to the drug company, draw up a new protocol, get ethical committee approval—'

'We'd have to work together,' David added in an ominous tone. 'Closely. Could you do that? With a *surgeon*?'

She seemed not to have heard the warning. Her eyes were shining again. 'It would be a fascinating project.' Her bottom lip was caught between small, even teeth. 'I'd like to try.'

'Good.' David dragged his eyes away from her mouth. 'So would I. We're agreed, then.' He held out his hand. 'Put it there, partner.'

It started as a handshake, an agreement between colleagues both excited by a shared new scientific horizon. But the movement of their hands died and it suddenly became something else. Their hands seemed as glued together as their gazes. Who looked away first? Who made the first move to withdraw from the physical touch?

Perhaps it had been simultaneous. As simultaneous as the knowledge that this voluntary physical contact had underscored something far more significant than a professional agreement.

The pile of background material was impressive. Lisa must have spent considerable time collecting the journal articles, textbook references and drug company data. It filled a large carton which David carried home with him the next evening. Deciding it was too late to begin his review, David then changed his mind a short time later.

The occupant of the next room had scored again. This one didn't giggle, but in a way her appreciative groans were worse. It made him think about what was going on far more graphically than he felt comfortable with. Gritting his teeth, David rummaged through one of his own boxes for his portable CD player and a disc of classical music. With the headphones on, the sounds of the activity next door were obliterated, but the music was not enough of a distraction to prevent him reading a few journal articles.

David reached for the top layer of journals, while making a mental note to try and catch sight of the stud who lived next door. With his determination to outdo Lisa in at least the hours worked in the hospital, he had spend the last weeks leaving too early and returning too late to meet his neighbour. It really was indecent that some junior doctor had both the time and energy for such a vigorous social life. It hadn't been like that in his day. David smiled wryly, settling back against the pillow on his single bed, a notebook, pen and journal to hand. Perhaps it had been—but those days were long gone.

It was only a recent discovery that they were a part of the distant past. Memories to file along with that of the delectable Miss Drummond. Mike had been responsible for the unsettling discovery with that double date he had organised with those cath lab nurses. They certainly had been great looking. Not to mention young, keen and ready for fun.

Why was it that neither he nor Mike had been remotely interested in taking them up on their unspoken offers? It had been almost funny, that embarrassing leave-taking at the nightclub, when the nurses had gone in one direction, with somewhat amazed glances at each other, and he and Mike had gone in another. David had tried to catch Mike's eye, ready to make some crack about it not being the best start to a bachelor career, but Mike had been strangely withdrawn and obviously not willing to discuss his lack of interest.

David had caught the mood, feeling somehow let down—with Mike and, more, with himself. The ingredients had all been there. Ten years ago he would have asked for nothing more. Now he realised that he needed something more but was unsure exactly what it was he was looking for. Maybe he should talk to Mike about it.

The journal forgotten, David checked his watch. Ten-thirty. He pulled his headphones off and reached for the bedside phone. It wasn't too late to call his old mate. It was time they had an evening out and few drinks. Just the two of them. They wouldn't include Gerry because he was too caught up in his own married bliss to understand. He and Mike needed a real talk so they could sort each other out and find out what it was they both really wanted out of life. It was Friday tomorrow, a perfect time for a well-lubricated philosophical discussion—something you couldn't have in feminine company. Forget marriages, babies and separations. Forget women in general and irritating cardiology registrars in particular. They were just strings, catches in an otherwise ideal existence. Maybe what he and Mike needed was just some good, plain, old-fashioned fun!

CHAPTER FIVE

'WHAT do you mean—you can't make it?'

David held the phone to his ear with his shoulder as he pulled up his jeans and fastened the stud. 'I've got it all arranged, mate. Pizza…beer. Hell, this pub's even got a wet T-shirt competition going.'

'Really? I didn't think they existed any more.'

'They're as rare as hen's teeth,' David warned. 'We might never get the chance again.'

'I can't. Listen, Dave, Anne's mother has just been admitted with an MI.'

'Are you treating her?'

'No, but Anne's on her way in and I can't leave.'

'Of course not. How bad is it?'

'Looks like a biggie. The paramedics had to jump-start her three times on the way in.' Mike hesitated. 'God, Dave, what am I going to say to Anne? We haven't even spoken to each other for three months and that was a blazing row about…about—'

'It doesn't matter what it was about,' David broke in. 'That was then. This is now. You'll know what to say, mate. This is Anne we're talking about, remember? The woman you loved enough to marry.'

'Yeah… I guess.' Mike still sounded dubious.

'I'm on my way,' David told him. 'You sound like you could use a friend and, to tell you the truth, I'd grown out of wet T-shirt competitions by the time I was sixteen.'

The bed nearest the main doors of the coronary care

unit had a clear view of the corridor that linked the wards and gave access to the lifts and stairwells. The occupant of that bed had more entertainment during the day, watching the varied hospital traffic, so it was a bed saved, if possible, for people who might appreciate a greater distraction from their situation.

David recognised the face of the patient in bed one as soon as he stepped from the lift. Stephen Taylor—the teenager in desperate need of the heart transplant. Word on the hospital grapevine had been that the initial approach to the potential donor's family had been unsuccessful, and the husband was now keeping a twenty-four-hour-a-day vigil by her life support system to prevent anyone turning it off. Staff were allowing the situation to continue in the hope that the family might come to terms with the decision that the inevitable termination of life support might be able to give hope to others.

Namely, Stephen Taylor. And Lisa Kennedy. Somehow David wasn't surprised to see the senior registrar sitting on the end of Stephen's bed. What was surprising was seeing her in jeans and a sloppy sweatshirt. A pile of classic car magazines was spread out on the bed cover. Lisa was off duty and using the time to enjoy a shared passion with another devotee.

'Look at that!' he heard her exclaim. 'Nice little MGB roadster. It's a 1967 model.'

'What year is yours?' Stephen's head was also bent over the picture in the magazine.

'Nineteen seventy-eight. But it's a V8. Talk about grunt!'

'Yeah, but look at this. That's for me!'

'An Alfa Romeo? In your dreams, kid.'

They looked at each other—the young doctor and the

teenager—and David felt his own heart squeeze painfully as he walked slowly behind Lisa's back. The way the boy looked! There was more than friendship there. More than a teenage crush. He was looking at a lifeline. And Lisa barely missed a beat.

'Hell, why not?' He could hear the smile in her voice. 'Dreams are free. But you might only be able to afford a Ferrari.'

'Not if he becomes a surgeon.' David couldn't help pausing. Lisa's head swung around.

'Not even surgeons earn enough for an Alfa Romeo 8c 2900,' she told him with gleeful certainty. Her curls bounced against her shoulders as she turned her head again. 'Stevie, this is David James. I told you about him.'

The boy looked suddenly even younger. Vulnerable. 'You're the guy that can do transplants,' Stephen Taylor said quietly.

'Sure can.' David stepped forward and laid a hand on Stephen's shoulder. 'I hope we're going to get much better acquainted in the near future.' He gave Lisa a quick sideways glance. Sitting there, in her jeans and oversized top, she looked almost as vulnerable as Stephen. The same mixture of doubt and hope crowded her expression and David had the ridiculous urge to gather them both up, to offer protection and comfort. And further hope. Instead, he allowed his gaze to be distracted by the hurried arrival of a newcomer.

'Anne!' he called.

The woman paused at the sound of her name and looked confused. The baby in her arms was crying. David excused himself and moved towards Anne just as Mike emerged from the curtained-off bed at the other end of the unit. They both seemed unaware of David's presence and spoke at the same time.

'Anne, I'm so sorry—'

'Mike, how bad is it?'

They both paused. Mike's face was a picture of concern. 'She's holding her own but it's quite serious. Would you like to come and see her?'

'Yes…of course… But…' Anne jiggled the red-faced baby, who was still crying loudly. They both appeared to notice David for the first time and again spoke as one.

'David! How good to see you!'

'Dave, would you mind, mate?'

David smiled and shook his head, holding out his arms. The baby was heavier than he had expected. Heavier, and distinctly damp. The baby took one look at his dismayed face and protested vigorously at her abandonment to someone so clueless. David moved quickly. A shrieking rugrat was not going to be welcomed by any of the unit's inhabitants.

Lisa and Stephen both watched him approach. They were both grinning from ear to ear.

'Suits you.' Lisa nodded. 'Shame *she's* not impressed.'

'Seems like I have trouble impressing a lot of females around here,' David muttered. He paused indecisively. 'Say, Lisa?'

'Mmm?'

'You couldn't give me a hand here, could you? It seems to have sprung a leak.'

This time he actually made Lisa laugh but David got no satisfaction from the accomplishment. He had been quite serious.

'Plumbing's your specialty, isn't it?' Lisa was still laughing. 'Sorry, David. I don't *do* babies.'

It was all too much. David stumbled from the unit, feeling totally useless and increasingly alarmed. The baby was going to damage itself, putting this much effort into trying to avoid his assistance. He found himself walking into the adjacent cardiology ward. He looked desperately into the first doorway he passed, hoping to find someone in a nurse's uniform. He needed help. He needed...Mrs Judd.

Funny how comforting a sea of pink candlewick could look. 'Mrs Judd? Do you know anything about babies?'

'I should do, dear.' The voice was wheezy but immensely reassuring. 'I've had eight of my own.'

Saturday morning was a good time to catch up with paperwork. It was also a good time to launch an unforgiving glare at Lisa during a quick visit to the CCU. He and Mike had postponed their drinks session in favour of lunch. Mike had made the suggestion himself late last night, having thanked David for caring for his daughter.

'It was no trouble,' David had assured him. And it hadn't been after he had discovered Mrs Judd. Cushioned on the wonderfully accommodating pink bosom, the baby had instantly succumbed to overwhelming exhaustion despite the wet nappy. Even after being returned to David's tense arms some time later, she hadn't woken, and David had strolled triumphantly back into the unit.

Damn shame Lisa hadn't been there to witness his success. And she certainly hadn't been prepared to lend a hand in adversity. The jeans had gone. Power dressing was back, high heels and all. So David glared and was rewarded only by a serene smile. His card was marked. Incompetent with cars, worse with babies. Mike didn't make him feel any better.

'Sorry, mate. I can't make lunch. I promised to babysit Sophie so that Anne can come in and visit her mother. She responded really well to the drug therapy. I rang Anne to tell her this morning and she was thrilled.'

Mike sounded thrilled himself. David wished he could share the happiness but his day was going steadily downhill. He left the unit, thinking that at least things probably wouldn't slide any further, but then the lift doors opened and he knew that they just had.

'Davey! I was looking all over for you.'

His younger sister, Melanie, bounced out of the lift and David's heart sank. If she'd come all the way to Christchurch, hunting for him, then she had to be in even more trouble than usual.

'Mel! You look great!' David resigned himself to his fate and held out his arms. And she *did* look great. Melanie was nearly as tall as he was. She had the same corkscrew curls but on her they were no handicap. She wore them long and very blonde and they had been a major drawcard during her brief flirtation with a modelling career. Big hair, which went with the same wide smile and a much less restrained personality. Already Mel had twisted out of his arms and had grabbed his hand.

'Where's your office, Davey? I've got something *really* important to tell you.'

'I'll bet.' David was grinning as he allowed himself to be towed along. 'It's that way.' Seven years Mel's senior, he had always enjoyed the role of older brother.

A steadying influence and, God knew, Melanie had needed one often enough. He cast a disapproving eye at the black leather mini-skirt and knee-high boots she was wearing. As for the cropped top—God, she'd even had her belly button pierced.

'*Mel!*' he gasped. 'You are unbelievable!'

'I know.' The unrepentant grin flashed. 'I love you too, Davey.'

Mel's voice had never been particularly quiet. David registered with some consternation just what it might do to his as yet unsalvaged reputation to be seen being enthusiastically dragged away by this startling woman. It took a while to get used to Mel. The thought was enough to make him glance over his shoulder as they passed the doors of CCU.

Stephen's expression suggested it was the most entertaining scene he'd witnessed for some time. Unfortunately, the expression on Lisa's face suggested something quite different. A faint groan escaped David's lips. It was all part of some conspiracy to turn his life upside down. Whenever he felt he was regaining his footing someone jerked the rug out from under him. And that someone was standing there beside her patient with the absolute confirmation of what she thought of him written all over her beautifully expressive face.

David had managed to forget the incident by the time Monday's workload was well under way. By that evening he was quite confident that Lisa's mood had nothing to do with him. She was, however, definitely miffed.

Her tone was clipped and formal and had been ever since they had begun their meeting an hour ago. She was also avoiding any eye contact. Something had upset her but David had no clue what it was and he wasn't about to ask. He caught enough flak from Lisa as it was. He wasn't about to step into her firing line.

Their discussion had gone very well and their proposed joint research project was shaping up nicely. Already they had agreed on entry criteria for patients and had categorised and ranked all the appropriate risk factors, such as advanced age, previous stroke, high blood pressure and diabetes.

'How clearly do you want to define cerebral damage?' David was scribbling notes. 'Another ranking system?'

'No. I'd rather keep that simple, the way I outlined in my original protocol. Two types. Type one—fatal injury, stroke, stupor or coma and transient ischaemic attacks.'

'And type two?'

'New deterioration in intellectual function. Confusion, agitation, disorientation, memory deficit or seizure without evidence of focal injury.'

'A lot of that is a bit arbitrary,' David pointed out. 'Some patients will experience things like agitation and disorientation as a quite normal result of major surgery and being in an intensive care situation.'

'I know.' Lisa sounded defensive. 'I've worked out a neurological checklist and time frame which should be able to distinguish anything significant. The focus for assessment will obviously be on the results of the CT scans.'

'What schedule did you have planned for them?'

'One prior to surgery, one at three days post-surgery and again at two and six weeks post-surgery.'

'And you got the go-ahead for that? Whew!' David whistled, impressed.

'Drug company funding is generous. They see acceptance of Neuroshield for clinical use as a priority. I've got the budget figures here.' Lisa reached for another manila folder in the pile beside her.

'Could you leave it with me?' David glanced at his watch. 'It's eight o'clock. Time we called it quits for today.'

'Sure.' Lisa rose to her feet instantly, as though glad of an excuse to escape his office. 'I hope I haven't made you late for anything.'

'Not at all.' David was watching Lisa as she gathered her folders. She was really quite tense but it didn't come across as her usual confrontational style. There was an underlying uncertainty that piqued his curiosity. Was she nervous about spending time out of hours alone in his office? Yet the meeting had been at her suggestion.

'I'm planning a quiet night,' he said cheerfully. 'I need to recover from the weekend.'

'I can imagine.' Lisa still didn't meet his eyes but David knew instinctively that he had stumbled on the reason for her disquiet. He wanted to prod a little deeper.

'Melanie is rather exhausting company,' he added. 'I didn't get much sleep.' He hadn't either. Melanie had bombarded him with talk of the new love of her life. An Australian opal miner who was absolutely *it*. There could never be anyone else as important to his sister's happiness. She was going to marry him. She knew this because he had called to invite her to visit him, on site, at one of his opal mines.

'Mmm.' Lisa's attention seemed to be very firmly focused on the papers she was sorting as she stood beside him. 'Yes. She looked rather…*energetic*. Here's the neurological checklists. You might want to have a look at them as well.'

David ignored the sheaf of papers deposited on the desk in front of him. Her tone had given the game away. Lisa was disapproving, to say the least. Of Melanie. He almost had the absurd impression that she was jealous. Surely not!

'It was rather an expensive weekend, too,' he found himself adding. Melanie had needed money for her desired trip to Australia and David had finally given in. He knew he should tell Lisa that Melanie was his sister but the very idea that Lisa might be rattled by his supposed relationship to another woman was intriguing. Very intriguing.

'I'm sure you got value for money.' Finally, Lisa looked directly at David. He held the eye contact, still musing over the underlying motivation for Lisa's disapproval. He wanted to spin the conversation out to allow more time for assessment.

'And you? Did you have a good weekend, Lisa?'

'Great, thanks. Sean Findlay and I went skiing on Mt Hutt.'

'*What?*' David was appalled. Lisa looked startled.

'What's so wrong with that?'

David swallowed hard. What *was* so wrong with that? Was *he* jealous? No way! And what business was it of his, anyway? Perhaps that was the sort of relationship Lisa wanted. If so, David needed to find out.

'Just how well do you know Sean Findlay, Lisa?'

'Well enough. He's been my registrar for a couple of months. He's good at skiing. We often catch a day on the slopes together.'

Skiing wasn't all Sean Findlay was good at. Should he tell her? He'd only found out himself this morning. David had been much later going in to work. His plan to drive Melanie to the airport had been thwarted by his car's refusal to start again, despite an expensive mechanical overhaul in the last fortnight. A taxi had been hard to procure in the rush hour and David had been kept late enough to finally meet the occupant of the neighbouring room.

David had eyed Sean with a new respect at the time. Now the thought of him alone with Lisa Kennedy was nothing short of horrifying. No. That wasn't the sort of relationship Lisa wanted. Look at the way she had dealt with Lewis's shallow advances.

'It's just…ah…' David hesitated. 'Some men, as you know, are only after a…a more shallow type of relationship.' He cleared his throat. 'I just wouldn't have considered him your type, that's all.'

'And what *is* my type?' Lisa enunciated very clearly. 'Someone like *you* perhaps?'

David felt inexplicably nervous. He had brought this on himself, playing games with the conversation. Lisa had managed to turn it in a very unexpected direction. Now, how the hell was he going to extract himself? The nervousness stemmed from an irrational desire to answer in the affirmative. Fortunately, he didn't get the chance.

'What's the problem here, David? Did Melanie have to go back to the library?'

'Sorry?' David was genuinely perplexed by the reference. 'No, she went to Australia. She was only here for the weekend.'

'And you have the nerve to accuse me of shallow relationships?' Lisa's smile was smug. 'Perhaps what is sauce for the gander, David James, should also be considered sauce for the goose.'

'But that's different!' David exclaimed.

'Why?'

'Because…because you're a woman.' David was actually shocked. Equality was fine. This, however, was unacceptable. 'Women are supposed to want more meaningful relationships.' And if Lisa didn't want something more, why hadn't she just played along with Lewis—and kept the bloody ring?

'Is that right?' Lisa sounded as though it was news to her. 'You forget, David. I'm a cardiologist, not a woman.'

'I give up.' David grinned, handing her the victory. 'You win—as usual.' She might have won a battle, certainly, but the picture of the whole war had shifted somewhat. David's grin widened a little. Lisa was jealous. Of Melanie! And he liked the idea. He really liked it.

'Shall we meet again, say, Wednesday evening?' he added quickly. 'After I've had time to peruse the budget?'

'Fine by me.' Lisa seemed happy to step off personal ground. The wind had gone from her sails and she looked vaguely disappointed. 'I'd like to get this sorted as soon as possible so we can get approval and get started.'

'We could go over it now if you like—over some dinner?'

'No.' Lisa looked up at the wall clock. 'I'm just going to look in on Stephen. He hasn't had a good day. It looks like his renal function is going downhill rapidly now.'

'Any word from Intensive Care?'

'Yes.' Lisa bit her lip. 'The woman's husband has come to terms with the idea that the life support system has to be switched off. He just wants one more night.'

'And?'

Lisa's lip trembled. 'He won't consider what he thinks of as further mutilation. No organ donation.'

David caught the single tear with his own thumb. Lisa's arms were full of manila folders and he couldn't bear the sight of that tear trickling down the side of her nose. The extra moisture still caught in her eyes made them shine.

Her voice was a whisper. 'I guess we can't win every battle.'

David was startled by her choice of words. It echoed too closely his own thought regarding their personal relationship. Lisa had won that one. And David didn't want her to lose this one either.

'We haven't lost yet, Lisa.' His thumb was still tracing the path of that tear. 'Not yet.'

His thumb had reached her lip. God, it was so soft! He could feel a remaining tremor. He could also feel an overwhelming urge to stifle the tremor with more than his thumb. He wanted to cover her lips with his own—to explore that extraordinary softness and mobility. David found his head lowering. He was so close he could almost taste her. It was Lisa's robust sniff that broke the spell. That, and her hurried exit from his office. David found himself walking after her—as though Lisa was stretching something between them that he couldn't bear to have broken just yet. He stopped just outside his office door.

We? David stared after Lisa as she headed down the corridor. Did I say, 'We haven't lost yet?' It wasn't his battle, was it? He wasn't involved, not really.

Damned right he was. David grabbed his white coat off the back of his chair. He was in it right up to his neck. And he was damned if they were going to lose. Not if he could help it.

Enter, stage right, cardiac surgeon. The hero of the hour. But David didn't feel like a hero. He felt humbled. It was an unusual sensation and he knew he looked far more serious than usual as he faced his small audience.

Stephen was propped up on a pile of pillows. An oxygen mask covered much of his face but didn't disguise the unhealthy, dusky shade to his skin, and it didn't detract from the expression his eyes conveyed. An expression that was mirrored on the faces of his parents, sitting quietly beside him. On the faces of three young women, presumably his sisters, and especially in the eyes of Lisa, perched on the end of Stephen's bed. David had eased himself through the closed curtains which had heightened his impression of enacting a drama. Now his audience was waiting and the spotlight had never felt so fierce.

He held up a single sheet of paper. 'This is a consent form for cardiac surgery.' His voice was uncharacteristically tentative. David swallowed and then spoke more firmly. 'Cardiac transplant surgery. We have a donor heart available.'

The silence and lack of any change in the expressions of his audience were nerve-racking. The air within the curtained-off area around bed one crackled with tension. David defused it as his slow smile broadened into a grin. Suddenly everybody was talking at once. Talking, laughing, crying and hugging each other. Arms only left one body to be wrapped around another. The sisters hugged each other, their parents and Stephen. They hugged Lisa. Lisa hugged Stephen's parents. David stood watching it all, a stupid grin still on his face. There would be time enough to arrange all the pre-operative details later. When it was Lisa's turn to hug Stephen it became too much. David felt the prickle of tears in his own eyes and moved to distance himself. He couldn't afford to become too emotionally involved at this point in time. Not when he was responsible for the surgery that Stephen and his family looked so eager to consent to. He mumbled some incoherent excuse and explanation that he'd be back shortly and ducked out from the scene. Out of CCU. David stood in the darkened corridor with his eyes shut, taking a few deep breaths. He felt someone's rapid approach but he was unprepared for the strength of the arms that wound themselves around his neck.

'David! Thank you. You're amazing!'

David smiled at the excited face so close to his own. 'About time you noticed, Lisa. You're not so bad yourself.' David's arms closed around her a little more firmly. He could feel the length of her spine, the softness of her breasts against his chest. He could feel the intense heat of the desire suddenly kindled at a much lower level. There was no way he could deny it now. He *wanted* this woman. He had to move. Now. Before she became aware of his body's reaction to her proximity.

Lisa unwrapped her arms the instant he moved. She hadn't noticed. She was still smiling happily.

'So, how on earth did you manage it? To get the husband's consent?'

'I'll tell you later. Right now we'd better get the ball rolling at this end. I need to go over the procedure with the family and get this consent signed.'

'Is Theatre booked?'

'Both of them.' David nodded. 'Seven-thirty a.m. tomorrow. Gerry's going to anaesthetise. Alan's going to assist me. Lewis was happy to delay his turn in Theatre.'

'*Was* he?'

David grinned. 'No. But I persuaded him.'

'You must be extremely persuasive.' Lisa was shaking her head in disbelief.

'Oh, I am. Just wait—you'll find out.'

David led the way back into CCU. He hoped she would find out. There had to be some way he could persuade Lisa into his life. God, into his bed at least.

There *had* to be!

CHAPTER SIX

'I THINK it's way past time we went to bed.'

'Exactly what I've been thinking.' David could feel the desire flickering. If Lisa looked up and caught his eye, he was sure it would explode into an unparalleled conflagration. Look up, Lisa, he urged silently. Never mind that it was nearly midnight and they'd both been sitting in a reflective silence as they'd finished yet another cup of coffee in the staffroom. He had never felt less tired in his life.

Lisa sighed wearily. 'You just can't help yourself, can you, David?'

'Sorry?'

'Flirting.' She did look up but her expression was a disappointment. No encouragement to fan the flames there. 'You just can't let any opportunity slip past. It's as automatic for you as breathing.'

'Some women appreciate it.'

'Oh, I know that.' Lisa's glance was as speculative as her tone. 'Don't think I haven't noticed the way nurses trip over themselves to be helpful. The right piece of equipment is always found, the patient's results are always available. *Your* patients are always in their beds and even the cleaner keeps the vacuum cleaner away while you're trying to examine someone.'

David grinned. He couldn't deny it. She'd left out his secretary, though.

'Even your secretary is a force to be reckoned with on your behalf,' Lisa continued acerbically. 'Do you know she pushed in front of me to get to the photocopier yesterday? Some reports that just *had* to be ready for you.'

'Did she?' David made a mental note to buy Sue a box of chocolates, while managing to look apologetic for Lisa's sake.

'*I'm* still waiting for discharge summaries which should have been typed up two weeks ago. And what about Mrs Judd?'

'What about her?'

'She wouldn't let me examine her this morning. She was hanging about, clogging up the corridor with her walking frame. It all became clear when she caught sight of you and had a chat. *Then* she was happy enough to relinquish her post.'

'I have *not* been flirting with Mrs Judd. We had a small bonding session, that's all—over a baby.'

'Well, it won't wash with me, David James, I'm warning you.'

'Why not?' David felt genuinely curious. 'This is a tough game, Lisa. It helps to lighten the atmosphere. You've got a sense of humour—I've heard you laughing often enough. What's so wrong with making people feel good about themselves, maybe feel attractive and appreciated.'

'Because you're playing on sexuality and you target women.'

'My inclinations *have* always been in that direction, I must confess.' David couldn't help smiling.

'It's chauvinistic and outdated,' Lisa growled. 'And it only makes it harder for women to succeed. How many female cardiology consultants do you know of, David?'

David thought hard. 'There's a brilliant woman at the Mayo Clinic and…ah…'

'Exactly. It's not an easy field for a woman. I intend to succeed, David. My career is my life. That's why I despise flirting.'

David had a flashback to their first meeting—to his husky comment about looking forward to working with her, to his crack about breaking her heart. He could write a manual on how to get off on the wrong foot with Lisa Kennedy. Yet she didn't seem to be berating him. It was more as if he was being pointed in the right direction. That was fine. He could modify more than his surgical technique. David was ready and more than willing to accommodate Lisa's preferences. Especially when they were explained so convincingly.

'Point taken. I hereby take the pledge to stop flirting.'

'Good luck.' Lisa was smiling. 'You might manage to cut down a bit where I'm concerned, anyway.'

'Being friendly never hurts. Look at the co-operation we've pulled together tonight on Stephen's behalf. I think we've got everything sorted now.'

Lisa nodded wearily but then her eyes widened with concern. 'Did you contact the blood bank?'

David nodded. 'Typed and cross-matched two units of whole blood and two units of packed cells, and we've got some platelets and fresh, frozen plasma on standby.'

'Did you get that last creatinine level through yet?'

He nodded again. 'His renal function isn't great, is it? We'll use a modified pre-transplant immunosuppressive regime with a reduced initial dose of cyclosporine.'

'Is Alan going to do the harvesting?'

'No, I'll do that while he gets Stephen onto bypass. Then I'll do the implantation. I can match things up better that way.'

Lisa was silent for a moment, then she sighed. 'It's wonderful for Stephen but it's a bit easy to lose sight of the other side of the coin. What's her name? The donor?'

'Stephanie Barry. Her husband's Greg. They've been married for three years, no children. She's twenty-five and worked in a pharmacy.'

'What happened?'

'A minor accident, really. They'd been out, celebrating Greg's promotion, and had had rather a lot to drink. Steph tripped over the front doormat when they got home and knocked her head on the doorhandle. She insisted she was all right, took some aspirin and went to bed. Must have had a severe intracranial bleed during the night and Greg was unable to wake her the next morning. He feels responsible now, of course. If only he'd taken her to a doctor. If only they hadn't had so much to drink—you know how it is. She's rather lovely, Stephanie. Long, black hair, at least what's left of it after the surgery...' David's voice trailed off.

Lisa broke the reflective silence. 'How *did* you get him to agree to the organ donation, David?'

'I'm not sure. After our meeting I wandered up to Intensive Care. I wasn't sure that there was anything I *could* do but maybe I just put myself in the right place at the right time. Greg wanted to talk. When he finally stopped I offered to tell him another story. He wanted to listen.' David gave Lisa a crooked smile. 'I gave him a version of your Wednesday lunchtime presentation. Not as well delivered as yours, but it seemed to be enough.'

Lisa nodded. Her smile was warm. 'Thanks again, David. It was a pretty special thing to do.'

'Do I get another hug?'

The look became withering. 'So much for the pledge, David James.'

'Sorry, I forgot. Only a momentary lapse, I promise.'

'Just as well you're not an alcoholic.' Lisa got to her feet and stifled a yawn. 'Sleep well, David. It's going to be a big day tomorrow.'

'Big' wasn't really the word for it. From the moment David set foot in the hospital, a mere six hours later, it seemed as if nothing else was going to happen that day which would be of any interest to anyone. The entire hospital was humming with the news that the first heart transplant in Christchurch was planned, and David began what he anticipated would be an emotional day with uncharacteristic apprehension.

His visit to Stephen Taylor and his nervous but excited family contrasted sharply with his next stop in the intensive care unit. There was no hope amongst the relatives of Stephanie Barry. There was a calm acceptance that only thinly covered the beginnings of a grief process which had, so far, been held firmly in abeyance, particularly by Greg. The visit had been difficult but David felt that Stephanie and her family deserved the dignity of her being treated like any other pre-operative patient.

This dignity was automatically extended by the staff in the theatre to which Stephanie Barry was delivered a short time later, still connected to her life support system. As David scrubbed, he could see through the window into the adjacent theatre where Alan Bennett was already under way, getting Stephen onto bypass. Gerry Greene gave a thumbs-up signal that made David smile as he reached for the sterile towel. Had Stephen

Taylor been conscious, no doubt he would have made an identical gesture.

Stephanie's theatre was crowded. A renal surgical team stood by ready to harvest her kidneys—David knew there were patients lined up to receive the organs later that morning. Theatre schedules had been disrupted hospital-wide but no one amongst the staff were grumbling, apart from Lewis Tanner. The atmosphere in this operating room was subdued but it didn't occur to David to request any background music. It was a grim task and one that they all wanted to complete successfully but as quickly as possible.

David made the initial long midline incision from the jugular notch to the pubis. As he began opening the chest, the renal team moved in to remove the kidneys. He glanced up as the renal surgeon requested a clamp, stating that he was about to clamp the renal pedicles.

'Start the heparin, thanks.' David nodded to the anaesthetist. 'And I'll have the cardioplegia needle.' It was placed in his hand and he inserted it into the ascending aorta and secured it. As soon as the blood-thinning properties of the heparin had taken effect, David signalled the anaesthetist to activate the pressure bag that would infuse the heart with the chilled cardioplegic solution. It took two minutes for sufficient cardiac cooling to occur and only a matter of a few more minutes for David to divide the main arteries and veins and remove the heart. The organ was placed in ice-cold saline solution and David led the way into the adjacent theatre.

His registrar and a volunteer general surgeon were going to close up and had assured David that the end result would be as visually acceptable as they could manage.

He couldn't afford to think about Stephanie Barry any more at this point. He had to concentrate on trimming and preparing the donor heart, a task that was carried out on a separate sterile table in Stephen Taylor's theatre. The marked change in atmosphere helped enormously. The positive side of the equation was paramount here.

When the preparations were complete, David moved rapidly towards the scrub room. He would have to re-scrub and re-gown, before starting the second part of the procedure—the removal of Stephen Taylor's heart.

He nodded at his assistant surgeon. 'That's great, Alan. You've cannulated the aorta in exactly the right place.'

'It was as high as I could make it. Are you ready for cross-clamping?'

David nodded again. 'Let's do it.' He concentrated fiercely on his excision, holding the memory of his trimming of the donor heart as closely as he could. The match needed to be as exact as possible.

'How are the haemodynamics looking, Gerry?'

'Great—pH is fine, arterial and venous saturation looking good. No problems at this end, Dave.'

David lifted Stephen's diseased heart clear of his chest cavity. It was carried away in a stainless-steel bowl that matched the one now on his trolley containing the healthy donor heart. David experienced a familiar jolt as he gazed briefly into the surgical field of Stephen's chest, devoid of the vital organ. This really was an extraordinary thing to do.

The atmosphere in Theatre changed again as David began the implantation.

'This is the easy part,' he told his team. 'Just a bit of fancy plumbing, really.' He broke the unusually tense silence he had been working in up till now and began a running commentary for the benefit of the large theatre team, none of whom had previously witnessed a cardiac transplant.

'We'll start at the level of Stephen's left superior pulmonary vein. Stay suture, thanks.' David placed the first temporary stitch. 'Now I'll have some double-armed 3.0 polypropolene and we'll use a whip stitch to join the left side of the atrial wall until we reach the septum.' He worked in silence for some minutes, tied the suture as he reached his starting point again, then held up the extra length of polypropolene.

'Cut, thanks,' he instructed the scrub nurse. 'Now we open up the donor right atrium,' he explained. 'I'm using a curvilinear incision up towards the appendage to avoid any later damage to the sinus node. Now we'll join up the right atrium. Suture, thanks.'

The whole team worked together brilliantly. David was very glad he had Gerry overseeing the haemodynamic status of his patient. It took a lot of the pressure off him and allowed him to concentrate totally on his careful suturing. The stitches were tiny and too numerous to consider counting. David was aware of his weariness as he worked to join the pulmonary arteries and the aortic openings. He straightened and pushed his shoulders back eventually, hearing a click in his neck which heralded some relief from the discomfort.

'Large-bore needle,' he ordered. 'Thirteen-gauge if you've got it.' He inserted the needle to evacuate air from the left ventricle of the heart. Turning his attention to extracting any air from the aorta, David ordered the removal of the cross-clamp as he applied strong suction to the needle vent. Air was taken from the right ventricle through the point at which the pulmonary arteries had been joined and the final suture was tied, with David confident that the danger of air embolism following the surgery had been minimised as much as possible.

Movement of Stephen's new heart had begun as David tied the final stitch, but it was uncontrolled and ineffective. A nurse stood by, holding the miniature paddles that were used for direct internal defibrillation, but David waited, watching the heart. It gave a more vigorous jerk of its own accord within thirty seconds and Gerry's voice was triumphant.

'We have sinus rhythm, folks!'

'We have lift-off.' David grinned. He raised a fist. *'Yes!'*

An excited buzz of conversation broke out. David nodded at the team of senior technicians who were responsible for the bypass technology.

'Start ventilation, Gerry. Let's get this lad off bypass. I'll have a wedge pressure, too, thanks. I want to assess cardiac function before we close up.'

At last it was over. Stephen had come through the major procedure with flying colours. He was well wired up for post-operative assessment but the care from now on would be routine, apart from the immunosuppressive drugs and reversed isolation nursing techniques.

David's stiff neck wasn't helped by the congratulatory back thump he received from Gerry and the vigorous handshaking from Alan Bennett and at least half a dozen others. With a pleasurable anticipation of a hot shower, David escaped the party atmosphere, noticing as he passed that the adjacent theatre was again in full swing as the first kidney transplant was being done. Still wearing his theatre gear, David went to the recovery room to check on Stephen. Lisa was already there.

'He looks great!' she told him excitedly. 'The family's all waiting outside. Could you talk to them?'

Of course he could. And did for some time. David still hadn't made it to the showers, however, as a small media contingent purposefully entered the waiting room.

'Could you give us a brief interview, please, Mr James?' The square end of a television camera moved in, the fluffy cover of a microphone hovering overhead. 'Tell us whatever you can about Christchurch's first cardiac transplant surgery.'

David hesitated. 'I doubt that the family wants any publicity. I must insist on the privacy of my patient being respected.'

'We don't mind.' It was Stephen's mother who spoke up. 'We feel like we're part of an historic occasion here. And it may be our only chance to thank the family of the donor.'

The camera changed direction.

'Could you repeat that, please, Mrs…?'

David couldn't escape it. Everybody wanted to offer congratulations. The bedside television sets of patients seemed to have his face on them every time he walked past. The flowers and cards that were pouring in for Stephen were causing problems for administrative staff, and even poor Greg Barry had been cornered by a television crew. David had felt very angry about that. Who had broken the rules of confidentiality? Too many people had been aware of the situation ever since Lisa had brought it to hospital-wide attention. Surprisingly, Greg had been as willing to talk as Stephen's family.

'It's actually helped me a lot, making that decision,' Greg explained to David when the surgeon had rung to apologise on behalf of the hospital. 'I don't mind other people knowing. Maybe it might help others to make the same decision themselves and let some good come out of tragedy.'

Certainly, hotlines had been set up and advertised on television for free phone calls to gain information about living wills, and a new debate began on whether an organ donation card system should be set up and incorporated into driving licences.

Stephen was doing brilliantly. His colour looked better than David had ever seen it and his renal function was already improving.

David escaped, late in the afternoon, to get some fresh air. The area of Hagley Park that bordered the other side of the river from the botanical gardens was a sea of daffodils at present. It was an inviting and relaxing environment which David shared with many other strollers, their children and numerous dogs. He was feeling much refreshed by the time he turned back to the hospital. Cutting through the staff car park, his eye was immediately drawn to the distinctive outline of Lisa's little red car. He ran an appreciative finger over the shiny paintwork and stooped to peer in at the low-slung seats. Only room for two people in that car.

'Fancy a ride, then?'

Lisa's breezy voice startled him. David stepped back a pace. 'Yeah, I would. But not right now, thanks. I've got rather a lot of paperwork. I want to write up my surgery report. Are you escaping?'

'Mmm. It's been a big day. I could do with a break. I might even get home in time to watch the news. I understand you're a media star as well now.'

David felt embarrassed. The cardiological side of Stephen's treatment until now had been ignored in favour of the drama of the surgery. The limelight had been all his. Again.

'Everybody's very impressed.' Lisa was selecting her car key from a full ring.

'Everybody except you.' David stepped closer again. Close enough to prevent her inserting her key into the door.

'Why should you want to impress me?' Lisa looked disconcerted.

'Damned if I know.' David stared at the face that had haunted his nights for weeks now. He'd better ignore the body, which had been even more of a sleep-killer. 'You're the most aggravating, opinionated and bolshy woman I've ever come across.' He took a deep breath. It was now or never. 'You're also the most sexually attractive, exciting and out-of-reach woman I've ever come across.'

Lisa's tone was matter-of-fact. 'You want to sleep with me.'

'Damned right I do.' But even as he rasped out the words David knew they came nowhere near expressing how he felt. Sleeping with her—that didn't cover it. Sex wasn't exactly it either. He wanted to be with her in a way he'd never been with any woman. And in a way she'd never been with any man.

'Why didn't you just ask?'

'Oh, sure.' David didn't like her cool appraisal of him. 'That would have gone down really well. Even better than flirting.'

'It would have been more honest. Who knows?' Something glinted in the brown depths to which David's gaze was locked. 'I might have said yes. Why don't you ask me now?'

'And become another notch on the old belt? No, thanks.'

'Isn't that what your sexual conquests have always been for you?' Lisa asked calmly. 'Chalk them up and get rid of them—in the nicest possible way, of course—if they get any ideas about something more. Sauce for the goose, David. Fair's fair.'

'This is different.'

'Why?'

'Because I feel different.' David put a hand on the door of her car. He wasn't going to let her make any attempt to escape just yet. 'I don't want to be a number. A slot on a time line between say…*ski* trips. I want it to be something special.'

'But you don't want something special.'

'How do you know?' David's voice rose. He was going out on a limb here in his admission. He felt torn by the desire to explain exactly how he felt, how important it seemed to be, but the fear of her reaction made it impossible. He was trying something that was costing him a lot of emotional effort right now. It was just typical of Lisa to want to argue about it.

'I overheard you talking to Mike the other day. He's rapt to be back with Anne and the baby. You listened to him rave on about the joys of marriage and the magic of kids with an expression like you were sucking on lemons.'

'I knew it was going to change things. I wouldn't get so much time with Mike.'

'So now you're looking for a new playmate. That's fine, but don't kid yourself that you want something special. You don't want marriage. You certainly don't want children.'

'Neither do you.'

'That's right. I don't.'

'So what's the problem, then? We're perfect for each other. I want you, Lisa Kennedy, and I think, maybe…' David leaned closer and noted her dilating pupils and quick intake of breath with satisfaction. 'I think, maybe, you want me, too.'

'Not on your terms.'

'What terms?'

'The ''something special'' terms. ''Special'' implies something worth keeping. A relationship that's allowed to develop and lead on into something more. Something more implies marriage…children.'

'Not necessarily.'

'In that case, ''something special'' implies a relationship that's going to cause a lot of pain when it's terminated.'

'Why should it be terminated?'

'Because there's no commitment. Why start something that's either going nowhere or going to end in disaster? It's something I've successfully avoided so far.'

David felt caught in a catch-22 situation. He couldn't win with Lisa if he offered any sort of commitment. He couldn't win with himself if he settled for anything less. 'And you intend to keep on avoiding it?'

'Yes.'

'Perhaps there's something else you should take into consideration.'

'Which is?'

'This.' David's hand snaked behind her neck, beneath the soft tumble of curls. The pressure he applied was gentle, but firm. At the same time he bent his head and his lips covered hers with a determination David had never before experienced.

He expected resistance—maybe a slap on the face or even a knee in the groin—but the fear of any consequences dissolved the instant his lips made contact with hers. They were softer that he had dreamed possible, the taste of her mouth sweeter. He had to taste more. David cupped her face in his hands, totally unable to prevent deepening the kiss. When her tongue flickered in response, David felt a wave of heat through his whole body. He was aware of her hands on his neck, her fingers in his hair. God, she wanted this as much as he did.

With a self-control David would never have believed he possessed, he broke off the kiss.

'Think about that, Lisa Kennedy.' His self-control even extended to making his tone nonchalant. 'If that's not something special then I don't know what is.'

If nothing else, the kiss had clearly given her food for thought. David did not seek out Lisa's company for the rest of the week. In fact, he was so busy that their planned meeting to discuss their research project on Wednesday night had to be postponed.

Media attention on Stephen Taylor had faded quickly and the teenager was doing extremely well. Mechanically ventilated in the immediate post-operative period, moved onto intermittent mandatory ventilation before transfer to the surgical intensive care unit, he had been weaned from assisted ventilation completely by the following morning. No bleeding problems had been experienced. Cardiac, respiratory and renal functions were more than satisfactory and Stephen was already talking hopefully about going home. Not that that would be a possibility for some weeks yet. Mike and Lisa had already done the first cardiac biopsy at three days post-surgery to check for any signs of rejection. The result had been excellent and the next of a series of biopsies was planned for the following week.

David's Wednesday morning theatre case was a patient from a different cardiology team, and he was under pressure from the respiratory side of his duties. A young patient with what should have been routine surgery for a minor lung lesion was experiencing complications that worried David. Already in the hospital well after hours, initiating a new course of treatment, David was kept even later when a major car accident sent him back to Theatre to attempt a repair on a badly crushed chest. They had to admit defeat at 4 a.m. and David returned briefly to his room without any hope of sleeping.

He felt dispirited. Another busy day was lined up tomorrow and even the weekend didn't promise any rest or relaxation. The conference in Queenstown was only a week away and David had still not prepared the paper he was expected to deliver. He was also lonely. He wanted someone to talk to about how he felt, losing the car accident victim.

He knew that the person who would understand best would be Lisa. Who else shared his passion and commitment to his career to the same degree? He knew nobody else who had avoided any distraction by a meaningful relationship in their private lives. Lisa would understand and that understanding would bring them closer together. Gerry was right. It was the bad times that really counted—that gave an opportunity for growth. The good times were the icing on the cake.

What good times? David snorted. One kiss? Lisa might be acting differently around him now, less confrontational, but there was a new wariness there as well. She hadn't given any indication that she might want to extend their professional relationship into something more personal and she'd made it sound as if that had been *his* decision when he'd been forced to cancel their planned meeting.

'Just let me know when you can fit it in,' she had said coolly. 'I'll make sure *I'm* available.'

Available. Ha! David sat on the edge of his bed, his shoulders slumped wearily. He rubbed his eyes, trying to remove the gritty sensation caused by lack of sleep. Available for sex, possibly. But that wasn't good enough for David. He wanted more. He wanted to be part of her life and for her to want his involvement in her life just as much. He wanted— God, *no*! David buried his face in his hands with a groan. He wanted to *marry* the woman!

'You're overtired,' he told himself, splashing liberal amounts of cold water on his face a few minutes later. Overtired and overwrought. It had been an extremely emotional week one way and another. But *marriage*! That was the last thing he wanted. The last thing Lisa wanted. He could just imagine her incredulous laughter if he voiced the suggestion. Or a caustic response along the lines of, 'Not in this lifetime, mate!'

David could feel angry, just imagining her response. He tried to turn the anger on himself. It had been his own bizarre idea after all. If he was stupid enough to even consider marriage before a first date had been agreed to then he deserved everything he got. No. He changed his mind and redirected his anger back at Lisa. Had this been the tack she had used to manipulate Lewis Tanner? Could that be why the infamous ring had appeared in the first place?

The solution was easy. Don't start anything, David warned himself. Men were supposed to be much better than women at letting their heads rule their hearts. He knew that the further the woman got under his skin the harder it would be to get over her. If her sexual promise lived up to that kiss then he would be a goner. And she had spelt out very clearly that she had no desire for 'something special'. It would be far preferable not to start anything than to get deeper in than he was already and then get dumped. David nodded with a resigned grimace as he reached to turn on the shower. That was it. He simply wouldn't let anything start.

But he knew, even as he let the needles of hot water erase his physical fatigue, that it was too late. The start had been made the instant he'd set eyes on Lisa, no matter how successfully he thought he'd denied it since. Now he was powerless to call a halt. The best he could hope for was a status quo and perhaps the natural death of an unnourished seedling. It was a technique he had used himself when he knew that a girlfriend had wanted more than he was capable of offering.

Now, for the first time, he could understand what they had gone through. He resolved, with a genuine determination this time, never to flirt again. The thought of past girlfriends was not cheering. Why couldn't he have fallen for one of *them*? Uniformly pleasant to be with, cheerful and eager to please. They had been ideal. *All* of them. Why, in God's name, did it have to happen with the most demanding, aggravating and challenging woman he'd ever come across?

One who didn't even want what he was capable of offering for the first time in his life. A commitment that would transcend a sexual liaison. A meeting of souls and not just bodies. Something that David knew, with a bitter realisation, that he would never have again to offer anyone else.

CHAPTER SEVEN

THE wariness was now mutual.

They were circling each other at a distance. When their orbits crossed there was a peculiar tension that seemed to David equally capable of exploding into a fracas or dissolving into wild, physical passion. Fortunately, the presence of other people prevented either outcome and David had been as careful as Lisa not to engineer any time alone together.

It had been quite easy to dictate the letter, outlining his approval of the budget for the research project, and send it on with the suggestion that Lisa organise the applications for clearance with the various authorities. Her response had been rapid, positive and also in writing. Perhaps they could conduct their entire collaboration by correspondence. It would take some time to get the go-ahead in any case and David had other things on his mind.

Like getting the medical illustrations department to make up the slides he needed for his presentation at next weekend's conference. He had almost reneged on his resolution to cut the flirting. The girl in medical illustrations had been ripe for a compliment on her ability to cope under pressure with maybe a special smile or appreciative glance. But David had held back. Instead, he sought out Alan Bennett as he came out of Theatre that afternoon and asked if he could throw his weight around as head of department to ensure the job was done on time.

'Of course.' Alan had nodded. He gave David a speculative glance as he ripped off his mask. 'I wouldn't have thought it would be any problem for you to have persuaded Ginette to cooperate. Are you feeling short on charm today?'

'Lisa has cured me.' David watched as Alan stripped off his gown and gloves, unaware of the despondent tone he had used. Lisa was right. Using sexuality as an advantage was chauvinistic and unacceptable. It was a potentially hurtful pastime and David had a new respect for the power of emotions. Unrequited lust was not to be recommended. It felt like a bad dose of flu—permeating every aspect of life. It helped to think of it as a viral illness. Maybe it was simply a matter of weathering it out. The symptoms would fade and with a bit of luck he would then be inoculated against a recurrence.

Alan was now regarding David with frank curiosity. 'Got time for a quick coffee?'

David followed his boss into the small theatre staffroom. They were alone as they helped themselves to coffee and biscuits. Alan broke the silence.

'What has Lisa cured you of, exactly?'

'Specifically—flirting.' David's grin was brief. 'Generally, I think I might be cured of believing myself to be more trustworthy than the average man is presumed to be.'

Alan's smile was thoughtful. 'Lisa's trust might be hard to win, but once you've got it, it's there for ever.'

David sighed. 'Why does she have to make it so bloody difficult, Alan? I know she's been let down but it's kind of insulting to be tarred by the same brush she used on Lewis Tanner.' He raised his eyebrows questioningly over the rim of his coffee-cup. 'How come you get to escape the mind set she has against men?'

Alan gave David a long, silent stare. Whatever he saw in David's expression seemed enough to end his indecision and he gave a slight nod. 'Lewis wasn't the first man to let her down.'

'Really?' His coffee forgotten, David leaned forward in his chair, eager to discover more. He knew so little of Lisa's background, and its importance suddenly seemed paramount. 'You know her pretty well, don't you, Alan?'

'I'm a father figure.' Alan smiled. 'Though she would be appalled if she heard me say that. She doesn't have much time for her own father.'

'Why not?' David prompted quickly.

'Lisa's mother died when she was quite young. Eleven or twelve. Her father wasted no time in replacing her, apparently. Lisa never got on with her stepmother.'

'Does she have any brothers or sisters?'

'Two brothers. They were quite a bit younger and had no trouble accepting a substitute mother. Lisa rebelled, her father supported her stepmother and Lisa gradually got pushed further out from the family. I doubt she'll ever forgive her father for what she sees as a complete betrayal—both of her mother and herself.'

'But that's well in the past. She's thirty-one—she must have been away from home for at least ten years.'

Alan nodded. 'She left home officially as soon as she started medical school but she'd been in boarding school for five years before that. There was an involvement at medical school. A much older student, I gather.'

'Another search for a father figure?'

'Maybe. It was very serious as far as Lisa was concerned. I don't know what happened but it was a disaster. He let her down so badly she told me once she had no intention of ever letting someone that close again.'

'And then there was Lewis.'

Alan nodded again but this time he smiled. 'Indeed. Though her methods of self-protection were well honed by then. He didn't hurt her as much as confirm her opinion of men in general. She's well armoured now.'

'You're telling me. Impenetrable barrier.'

Alan spoke carefully. 'She might like to think it is but I know differently. She's got a great deal to give the right person. If she gets hurt again she might be able to lock it away for ever.' He gave David a sharp glance. 'Don't hurt her, David. Lisa is a very special woman.'

'I'm aware of that.' David lowered his voice as several nurses entered the room. 'I have no intention of hurting her.' He rose slowly to his feet and picked up his cup of now cold coffee and an untouched biscuit. He shrugged. 'I don't think I'm going to get the chance, anyway.'

The woman from the administrative offices might also have responded to a bit of flattery but David knew he was cured when he didn't even think of trying. The month of temporary accommodation in the junior staff quarters had expired a week ago. Some overseas junior doctors were arriving within a fortnight and Administration was obliged to provide accommodation for them. Could he please make sure his room was available by then?

David had assured the woman he could—and would. What was one more hassle after all? Moving away from being Sean Findlay's neighbour would probably be beneficial. David had been astonished at the way he had shot across to his door and opened it last night, on hearing voices as Sean unlocked his door. He had peered around the edge, feeling ridiculously childish, but the relief of finding that Sean had not persuaded his senior registrar to experience the delights of his nocturnal company had made it worthwhile at the time.

The ecstatic postcard from Melanie which had arrived on his desk that morning had rubbed a little more salt into the wound. Her love was very far from unrequited, though no wedding arrangements were forthcoming quite yet. They were taking a trip to the Great Barrier Reef shortly—a much more conducive setting for a proposal.

Queenstown would be, too, David had thought suddenly. He'd had a vivid image of flying down a snowy slope on skis, Lisa keeping pace with him…just. He would stop with a spectacular flourish that would send a huge spray of sparkling snow against the brilliant clear blue of the sky, lift his goggles and shout, 'I can't possibly live without you, Lisa. Marry me!'

David shuddered. He certainly had a bad dose. Just as well he didn't know the first thing about skiing. And, according to Mike, Lisa was still undecided about whether she would even attend the conference.

'I imagine the recreational activities on Sunday morning will tempt her along,' he told David on Wednesday afternoon as they were both preparing to leave work.

'I haven't seen the programme for social events.' David leaned back against the corridor wall. 'What's on offer?'

'What isn't? Skiing, bungee jumping, a deer park and historic village tour, four-wheel-drive trip to the historic mining settlement at Macetown. The Shotover jet-boat ride or a trip out to the Skippers Canyon.'

'Wow. There's more on the social agenda than the clinical side.'

'Of course.' Mike grinned. 'Why else do we all go to these things?'

'I suppose Lisa will go skiing.' David damped down the replay of his fantasy.

'More likely bungee jumping. She's a great one for picking something risky.'

'Really?' She wasn't prepared to take a risk on *him*. After his conversation with Alan Bennett, David could understand that the possibility of serious physical injury was less offputting than an emotional equivalent. Right now, David felt inclined to share the preference.

The sight of Lisa, following a new arrival through the coronary care doors, caused a now familiar sinking sensation mingled with the pain of a very frustrated desire.

'Not for me, though,' Mike was saying. 'I know exactly where I plan to spend Sunday morning.'

'The deer park?'

'No way, mate. I'll be in the same place I'll spend Saturday night after the conference dinner. In bed.'

'Sounds restful.'

'Don't you believe it. Anne's coming too.'

'Is she?'

'You bet. Things are better than they've ever been, Dave. Her mum's doing really well at home now and Anne's sister is coming down for the weekend and will look after Sophie as well. It'll be the first time we've had to ourselves in a very long time. It's going to work out—I know it is. We both know it.'

'That's great.' David smiled at Mike's obvious delight. 'Hey, I've just thought of something. That flat you've been in while you were separated—can I take it over? I've got to move out of the staff quarters next week.'

'Sorry, mate. The landlord had someone lined up the day I handed in my notice.'

'Oh.' David's face registered his disappointment. Then his expression changed. The corridor outside the doors of CCU had suddenly filled with a small group of people, including a woman in a wedding dress. David's jaw dropped. First he spotted Lisa and now he was faced with the sight of a bride looking like a giant meringue, full-length dress, veil, bouquet and all. There was just far too much of it around. Why couldn't people get on with their lives, without messing them up with archaic concepts like marriage?

And why did he seem totally unable to avoid his own preoccupation with it? He knew why, of course, and the thought of Lisa wearing a fluffy white creation like that was ludicrous enough to make David laugh aloud and ease the tension he felt. Mike turned his head at the sound in time to see the numbers in the group increase. The volume of their agitated conversation also increased. There was more than one argument in progress.

'Come on. I can't wait to find out what this is all about.' Mike strode down the corridor. 'Could I ask you all to move into the relatives' room, please, folks? We need to keep the noise level down a bit. We've got some rather unwell people nearby.'

The bride burst into tears. 'You mean Daddy, don't you? He's going to die!'

The young man in the grey morning suit glared at her. 'Well, don't blame *me* if he does.'

'He didn't want me to marry you in the first place.'

'We're not married yet—thanks to your father's histrionics.'

'Are you suggesting my husband pretended to have a heart attack just to interrupt your wedding?' An older woman in a beige suit with a matching hat leaned forward and poked the young man in the chest. 'How *dare* you! George was right about you all along.'

'Please!' Mike said loudly. '*This* way. All of you.'

The group shuffled sideways reluctantly. David was watching it all in total amazement. His eyes focused on the man who put an arm around the groom's shoulder.

'Don't I know you?' David queried.

'No,' the man answered quickly. 'I don't believe we've ever met.'

Another young man in the same attire as the groom looked at David curiously. 'Have you bought a car recently?'

'I wouldn't call it a car exactly.' David grinned. 'More of a conversation piece. It doesn't go.'

'That'd be right. And you probably paid five times as much as it's worth.'

'The man's a crook!' someone called.

The woman in the beige suit nodded emphatically. 'Talk to my husband, George,' she advised. 'If he recovers.' She sighed heavily. '*He* could sell you something decent—at an honest price.'

Mike had stopped trying to move the group. He was barely able to suppress a smile. Lisa strode out of the CCU doors at that moment.

'Just *what* is going on out here?' she demanded.

'Ah, Dr Kennedy.' The beige suit moved away from David. 'It was so lucky you were on duty today. So nice for George to have someone he knows from the Classic Car Club. Can I see him now, please? Is he going to be all right? It's all the stress, you know. It's just been too much for all of us.'

'He's going to be fine, Mrs Hammond. It looks like it's a severe attack of angina. We can't find any evidence of a heart attack. It's a shame he forgot to take his medication to the wedding.'

'I told you!' the groom snarled. 'He was just trying to foul things up yet again.'

'And he was right!' the bride sobbed. 'You only want to marry me so you can work in a decent business. It was all your father's idea.'

'Well, I never!' Another middle-aged woman, in a pink dress, clutched her matching handbag to her chest. 'I told you she wasn't good enough for you, Dwayne. Selling BMWs has made the whole family into unbearable snobs.'

'That's what you need.' The best man nodded at David thoughtfully. 'A BMW. Dad's probably got just the thing. You can get rid of the bucket of rust Clive here has ripped you off with.'

'I don't rip anyone off. And I don't put ridiculous mark-ups on cars that decent folk can't afford anyway.'

'Cheap rubbish, that's all you sell. Only fit for the scrap yard.'

Lisa was looking stunned. Mike was now grinning openly. The bride was sobbing uncontrollably and David watched her with some interest. He couldn't see any indication of vital orthodontic work needed.

'I guarantee satisfaction,' Clive stated loudly. He put his hand on David's shoulder. 'If you want your money back on your car, young man, you can have it. Every penny.'

'Well…I…' David caught Lisa's eye. She was now standing between the hysterical bride and Mrs Hammond. She was trying hard not to laugh.

'Take it quick. You've got witnesses,' a new voice broke in loudly.

'Shut up, Doreen. This has got nothing to do with you.'

'Don't you tell me to shut up. You know perfectly well your brother's as crooked as they come. And you're not much better—falsifying your tax return.'

'Doreen, shut *up*!'

'And I'll bet your nephew got that girl pregnant on purpose. It's all about money, isn't it? It's all your whole family cares about.'

'I'm *not* pregnant!' the bride wailed. 'I only *thought* I was.'

'That wasn't why we're getting married,' the groom added. 'I love Charlene. She loves me.'

'No, I don't. Not any more. I don't want to marry you.' The bride wiped her nose on her sleeve. 'I want to see Daddy.'

'So do I.' Mrs Hammond's arm was firmly around her daughter. 'He's going to be so happy about this, darling. You'll see, it's all for the best. And don't you worry about the cost of the reception. It doesn't matter a bit.'

David's gaze hadn't left Lisa's throughout the last rapid-fire exchange between the acrimonious group. They were both smiling but now it had nothing to do with the farce being enacted around them. They were smiling at each other, enjoying each other's amusement. David felt a wash of emotion much deeper than amusement. A feeling of caring about how someone else felt which was entirely selfless. A warm, melting sensation that went right through him.

Instinctively, he recognised the unfamiliar sensation. He wanted to throw his own voice into the babble of arguments they had been caught up in. He wanted to shout, 'I love you.' Or at least mouth the words now that he had made what seemed to be the most exciting discovery ever. The whole situation was so ridiculous it was almost appropriate, but even as David opened his mouth Mrs Hammond used her free hand to grip Lisa's arm.

'Take us to George, Dr Kennedy. He needs us.'

The white veil floated behind the women. Clive, the car dealer, looked at the groom.

'I guess that's that. Let's go and have a drink, son.' He didn't look back at David. 'You wouldn't want to hock off BMWs anyway. Where's the challenge in that?'

Mike ushered the remaining Hammond relatives into the waiting room. He nodded at David as he closed the door behind him.

'I'd better go and make sure George is coping with the excitement of the news.' He smiled. 'Want me to put in a word for you?'

'About what?' For an insane second he thought Mike was offering to let Lisa know what he had discovered.

'A BMW.' Mike laughed. 'Doesn't pay to pass up a good opportunity. You could have got your money back there.'

'I'm not bothered,' David assured him. And he wasn't. At least not about missing that opportunity. He wasn't going to carry on avoiding Lisa's company, however. Any opportunity that presented itself in that direction he was going to grab with open hands. Somehow he was going to persuade Lisa that he deserved her trust. And when that happened he was going to make damned sure he never let her down.

The conference in the Central Otago tourist destination of Queenstown should have provided any number of such opportunities, but by Sunday morning David was despairing of finding any at all.

He had flown in early on the Saturday morning on the chartered flight, catering for a large number of the conference delegates, disappointed that his searching hadn't revealed Lisa to be one of the passengers. Perhaps she had decided against coming after all. They had all been ferried directly to the conference venue and the pace had been relentless for the rest of the day. Presentations, satellite meeting and panel discussions had run back to back. The cardiology side had run parallel to the surgical interests, but David's presentation had been part of a combined session that had run for the first half of the afternoon.

David was between Mike Foster, presenting a physicians' perspective of diagnosis and treatment, and another cardiologist, looking at the haemodynamic and angiocardiographic considerations of the congenital heart condition of tetralogy of Fallot. David was well prepared to update delegates on the advances in surgical treatment. The three speakers would then form a panel to answer any questions from their audience. The discussion at the conclusion was lively and it was only then that David spotted Lisa in the packed auditorium, sitting near the back, beside Alan.

The drug companies funding the conference outdid themselves in preparing the Saturday evening entertainment. Black tie had been requested and David was still fumbling with a cufflink as he arrived, having had to rush to shower and change following the final satellite group he had attended.

The hotel venue was lavishly decorated with hundreds of red, heart-shaped balloons. The numbers of people had nearly doubled as partners had joined the delegates and David was disappointed to find the seating pre-arranged to mix the representatives from the various centres. David was at a table with an Australian surgeon and his wife, an Auckland cardiologist, who was accompanied by his wife and daughter, and a registrar from Dunedin who was, like David, without a partner.

Mike and Anne were at a nearby table and David was aware of a distinctly unpleasant wave of jealousy when he saw that Alan and Lisa were also sitting together as partners. Lisa looked stunning. Her hair was piled up in some kind of a loose knot arrangement that allowed a few curls to escape and, in David's opinion, rather too much of a beautifully tanned skin was revealed by the shoestring straps and high hemline of the elegant black dress she wore. David poked at the heart-shaped terrine they had received as an entrée and wondered if he was going to enjoy the evening after all.

He had little choice. A popular street theatre group had been engaged for entertainment and they had unearthed or invented a whole new field of hilarious jokes and stories about doctors in general and cardiac specialties in particular. Many of them were acted out and audience participation was demanded and became more enthusiastically offered as the evening wore on and the waiters tirelessly refilled champagne glasses.

The dessert of strawberries, ice cream and tiny heart-shaped biscuits had barely been cleared away when each table was presented with a bag of objects. They had to devise a new or improved version of a heart operation and then demonstrate it to the rest of the gathering.

David was soon caught up in playing with the balloons, straws, paper clips and string they had been provided with. He thought his group had done a creditable job of revising a mitral valve replacement and it was amusingly presented by the Australian surgeon, but it was Alan's group that got by far the biggest laughs. They had added one of the red, heart-shaped balloons to their booty, which Lisa held clutched to her chest. She lay on their table as Alan seriously explained the highly unlikely theory behind their new method of balloon angioplasty.

Even David was convulsed with laughter as the red balloon popped unexpectedly and the street theatre group joined in as a voluntary transplant team.

It was after midnight as the gathering broke up. David saw Mike and Anne hurry away, hand in hand. He hadn't even had a chance to speak to Lisa but she and Alan were now surrounded by a laughing group, congratulating them on their impromptu presentation. Frustrated and suddenly weary of the whole event, David slipped away to his room.

The foyer was beginning to fill up with people when he came down again the next morning. David scanned the lists for the recreational events on offer. He wanted to know what Lisa was planning. Groups were already on the move to board the line of buses parked outside the main entrance to the hotel. Bungee jumping was surprisingly popular and the Shotover jet-boat excursion was fully booked. He was too late for the four-wheel-drive trip to Macetown and there was no point in going up Coronet Peak for the skiing. David spotted the names of both Alan and Lisa on the trip for the Skippers Canyon. Hurriedly, he added his own name, taking the only slot still vacant for the six-seater minibus. He would be playing gooseberry but that was preferable to having no time with Lisa at all.

The driver, a man in his forties with a cheerful smile and a cowboy hat, was leaning against the minibus, smoking a cigarette. David thought he would be the first passenger to board the vehicle but the driver grinned at him.

'Good-oh, another customer. I was beginning to think you'd all chickened out.'

It would be Lisa who had beaten him to it. Typical! Not only that, she had taken the seat with the best view, alongside but slightly behind the driver's seat. It gave a clear view through the front windscreen.

'Hi.' David greeted her casually. 'I thought you'd be hitting the slopes with your penchant for skiing.' He hadn't intended any innuendo but Lisa's expression tightened noticeably.

'I can ski anytime. Besides, it gets very boring, repeating the same activity endlessly.'

'Does it?' David's query was polite but he wasn't inclined to agree. He could think of one activity he wouldn't mind repeating for the rest of his life—as long as his partner was the woman he was now seated next to. 'Oh, sorry,' he added quickly. 'Were you saving this seat for Alan?'

Her glance was curious, her voice a little unsure. Was she as aware as him of the contact their thighs were forced into by the width of the seat?

'Alan's not coming after all,' Lisa told him. 'He's got a bit of a hangover after last night.' She looked away and seemed to take a deep breath. 'Sit wherever you like.'

'I like it here,' David said mischievously. He settled himself a little more comfortably. Lisa looked studiously out of the window but didn't try and edge away from the now firmer contact of their legs.

David's Auckland cardiology companion from last night's dinner strode towards the minibus driver. His voice carried through the open door.

'Look, I'm sorry about this but someone's just warned my wife off from doing this trip. She has a fear of heights and we had no idea that the road was so primitive. She and my daughter have decided to go for the deer park trip. I'll have to go with them.'

'No worries,' the driver said. 'It's all paid for, anyway.' He leapt aboard the bus and smiled broadly at his only passengers. 'We'll be able to go a lot faster with fewer people on board. Either of you two want to chicken out and give me a morning off?'

David and Lisa both shook their heads. Their driver sighed theatrically and flopped into the driver's seat. 'Spread yourselves around, then,' he invited. 'There's stacks of room.'

David and Lisa both stared out through the windscreen as the bus lurched and then picked up speed. Neither of them moved.

'My name's Harry.' The driver seemed to take his eyes off the road for a considerable length of time as he tugged his hat in his passengers' direction. 'Had to give up being a ski instructor when I broke my legs. Boy, I miss those ski bunnies, but, hey! This is much more exciting.'

Lisa's eyebrows had been rising steadily. She caught David's eye and he grinned.

'Is there something about this trip I haven't been told?'

'I believe it's rather spectacular. Somebody did mention hair-raising.'

'You can always hold my hand,' David invited. He

expected a rebuff—an exasperated look at the very least—but Lisa's mouth curved just a little.

'I'll keep that in mind.'

David stared at her profile. He was rather tempted to take the hand lying in her lap anyway but Harry's enthusiastic wave towards the side window distracted him.

'Look at those suckers!' Harry crashed down through the gears and slowed the minibus.

David and Lisa looked. The ancient bridge spanned a deep, narrow gully and was crowded with people. As they watched, a figure fell from the bridge and they could hear a scream of pure terror. The bungee line attachment curved behind the rapidly descending body until the slack was taken up, but the body kept falling until almost at water level as the line stretched. They heard another scream as the person was jerked back up on his first bounce. Harry pulled away again.

'Beats me why they line up to do it,' he announced cheerfully. 'Bloody dangerous.'

Within minutes, David began to wonder whether he and Lisa had, in fact, chosen a safer option. With only room for one vehicle, the winding, unsealed road was carved into the edge of the Skippers Canyon. He couldn't see the edge of the road from his vantage point but he could see the spectacular drop of what seemed thousands of feet to where the Shotover river snaked through the depths of the canyon.

Harry had gone into tour-guide mode. 'If you put the Shotover together with the Arrow River and Skippers Creek, you've got one of the highest densities of gold-bearing gravel in the whole world. The original road was made in 1863. You can still see a bit of it over there.' He waved towards the side window again but David was relieved that he kept his own eyes on the road. Perhaps he wasn't quite as casual about his responsibilities as he seemed.

'How much traffic does this road get?'

'Heaps. 'Specially over summer.'

'What happens when you meet something coming the other way?' David asked cautiously.

'One of you has to back up. There's the odd place you can pass.' Harry laughed. 'It's good fun. We have to watch out for rock falls as well and slips can be a problem when it rains.' He leaned forward and looked up. 'Looks like rain, now,' he remarked happily. 'Or snow, maybe. But don't worry. I've got enough shovels for all of us in the back.'

They stopped briefly to admire some of the old gold-working sluices and a little longer at a small museum. The weather was, indeed, beginning to look a little threatening with black clouds edging out the huge fluffy mounds of cumulus. Then it was on to the main tourist attraction of the ride, the astonishing Skippers suspension bridge.

'The original bridge was built in 1868 and was replaced by this one in 1901. It hangs ninety metres above the river, which makes it the highest suspension bridge in the country.'

David and Lisa had climbed out of the bus again and were following Harry along the bridge on foot.

'The span is ninety-six metres and the towers are eleven point five metres high and made of concrete, which was an unusual building material here at the time.'

It was incongruous, the magnificent bridge at the end of a tortuous road to nowhere.

'Why did they build it?' Lisa queried, echoing David's thought.

'The Bullendale Mine was the big industry—up at the head of Skippers Creek. Site of New Zealand's first hydroelectric plant in 1885, but it was already in decline by the time they built this bridge and it closed only six years later.' Harry laughed with genuine pleasure. 'Typical political miscalculation, I guess. The ratepayers are probably still footing the bill.' Harry checked his watch. 'We'd better head back. We're going to get dumped on pretty soon, and don't you guys have a plane to catch at one?'

David nodded but Lisa shook her head. 'Not me,' she said. 'I prefer to do my own driving.'

'Cool.' Harry flicked a cigarette butt over the side of the bridge. 'You can drive back if you like. How's your insurance?'

Lisa laughed. 'Not that good. I'll pass, thanks.'

They sat together in the bus again. It seemed silly to take different seats on the return trip. David was thoroughly enjoying the rough surface of the road and he allowed his leg to rest a little more heavily against Lisa's. The trip wasn't quite as nerve-racking, going in the opposite direction, as the sheer drop was now on Harry's side of the road. Harry put the windscreen wipers on as the first heavy drops of rain hit the windshield. He changed into a lower gear as they began to move up a sharper incline. Whistling 'She'll be Coming Round the Mountain', he seemed perfectly happy until the thunderstorm broke.

The fork of lightning was more spectacular than anything a tourist company could have laid on. It seemed to be pointing into the canyon right beside them and the instantaneous clap of thunder demonstrated how close it was. Lisa jumped and her face paled. David was equally startled but the effect it had on Harry was cat-astrophic.

'Bloody *hell*!' he exploded. Then his face lost any vestige of colour and he collapsed forward onto the steering-wheel in an apparent dead faint. His foot fell off the accelerator, the bus gave a jolt, stalled and began a backward drift down the incline.

David's expletive was just as forceful as Harry's had been. He was out of his seat and hauling Harry back from the wheel before he had time to draw another breath. Lisa's face was now white. She was terrified. The bus was picking up speed in its backward slide and was heading towards the edge of the precipice.

David held the unconscious driver back with one arm and made a grab for the handbrake. The bus slowed but continued to slide. His face set with grim determination, David took hold of the steering-wheel and pulled. The bus turned only a fraction then it leaned to one side— the side with the drop into the canyon. Lisa gave a stifled scream but David was again pulling forcefully on the hand brake. Finally the backward movement ceased. The van teetered for a second and a horrified, still silence fell.

David pulled the lever that opened the door. He put his hands under Harry's armpits and began to drag him clear. The van seemed to lean sideways as the internal weight shifted and Lisa sat, frozen, her knuckles white where she gripped the bar in front of the seat.

David was back within seconds. He came only half-way up the steps, leaning forward so that he was only inches from Lisa's pale face. He laid his hand gently on her cheek.

'Come on, love,' he said calmly. 'I need you.'

The bus teetered again as Lisa stood up. It was a

small movement but her eyes widened with renewed fear. David reached out and took her in his arms, lifting her clear of the bus.

'It's not going to fall,' he told her. 'We've got one wheel that's a bit off the road, that's all.'

'That's all?' Lisa's voice was a squeak. David allowed her to cling to him for just a second longer.

'Harry needs some help,' he whispered in her ear. 'He may have had a heart attack. He needs a *real* doctor.'

Somehow Lisa managed to laugh and fight off her shocked paralysis. David was proud of the way she turned her attention to Harry's plight. It seemed far too long since the emergency had begun but Harry's face was only now changing colour to indicate a dangerous lack of oxygen. It had been little more than a minute since he had collapsed.

Lisa launched into vigorous CPR, having checked Harry's airway. She directed David's chest compressions as she breathed for their patient. After several minutes Lisa told David to pause as she laid a hand on Harry's neck.

'We've got a pulse,' she said excitedly. She put her ear close to Harry's face. 'And he's breathing.' She sighed in frustration. 'I wish I had an ECG going on him right now.'

'Do you think he has had a heart attack?'

Lisa shook her head thoughtfully. 'It was an extremely sudden collapse. No hint of chest pain or sweating or nausea.'

'Maybe he's got hypertrophic obstructive cardiomyopathy—like Wayne Drummond.'

'Could be. Or possibly something like long QT syndrome with an arrhythmic reaction to a sudden shock. That lightning gave him a hell of a fright.'

'He wasn't the only one,' David muttered.

Harry was still unconscious but David smiled at Lisa's triumphant expression as she rechecked his vital signs. Then his smile faded abruptly. He could hear the sound of an approaching vehicle that would not be able to see them around the tight bend. Springing to his feet, David began to run uphill, signalling frantically as he began the turn.

The driver of the other minibus was a mate of Harry's. He looked shocked. His expression was mirrored by the full busload of Japanese tourists staring from the windows of his bus.

'Is he going to be OK? Has he had a heart attack? I've been telling him to quit smoking for years!'

'We need to get him to hospital as fast as possible,' Lisa stated. 'We're not sure what happened yet.' Lisa was watching over a now conscious but very subdued Harry.

'I've already called for help.' The second driver patted the mobile phone clipped to his belt. 'Search and Rescue are on their way with a Jeep.' He walked a few steps and stared yet again at the wheel of their bus which was, in Lisa's opinion, a lot more than a little way off the road. Words failed him and he simply shook his head and whistled silently.

'Do you guys have any idea of just how lucky you are?'

David and Lisa stared at each other. It was Lisa who spoke quietly.

'I think we do, don't we, David?'

'Oh, yes.' David agreed wholeheartedly. 'I think we know exactly how lucky we are.'

*   *   *

'Next time, we'll go bungee jumping.'

'Absolutely. Much safer.'

'You saved my life, David.' Lisa's eyes darkened at the memory of horror but her face was now quite calm. They were standing outside the doors of Queenstown's small hospital.

'And you saved Harry's. I would have picked a heart attack as first choice but you were right. Long QT syndrome. Prone to arrhythmias and cardiac arrest under emotional stress. I wonder whether he'll be transferred to Dunedin or up to us in Christchurch for further tests and treatment.'

'I wonder.' Lisa was watching a small plane begin its ascent, having taken off from the airport close to the hospital. 'You've missed your flight,' she commented.

David grinned. 'I was going to ask you for a lift, anyway. I fancy a ride in a fast, red car.'

Lisa returned the grin. 'I was going to offer you one, anyway. You didn't have to save my life in order to get it.'

'Oh, yes, I did.' David's hand cupped Lisa's chin.

'Why is that?' She was still smiling.

'I was saving my own life as well, Lisa. Without saving you, that would have been a little pointless.'

Lisa's eyes were locked with his. 'You were right, David. You *are* something special.'

David's lips were nearing their target and he didn't reply. His kiss was tender. It wasn't the time or place to unleash the passion that Lisa's response confirmed was reciprocated. He could wait. But not for too long.

'Let's go, Dr Kennedy. Take me home.'

CHAPTER EIGHT

NOTHING had ever felt so good.

David dared not move, even to ease the cramp in his left leg. Lisa lay curled against him, her head buried in the hollow of his shoulder, her arm flung across his chest. He could feel the tiny puffs of her breath, stirring the hair on his chest, and he was aware of his nipple tightening in response. That wasn't all that was tightening but surely he couldn't expect her to want any more just yet?

They hadn't even stopped to eat when they'd arrived at Lisa's small town house early last evening. She had led him straight into her bedroom without saying a word. David hadn't dared break the silence for fear of breaking the spell that had allowed this miracle to happen.

It had been a revelation. He had guessed at Lisa's passionate nature and had known how good it would be, but David had had no idea of the difference in his own response. For the first time he'd realised what it was to really make *love*. More concerned with Lisa's satisfaction than his own, it had had the unexpected effect of making his own overwhelmingly more intense. The memory only raked the embers of the desire he had woken with and he stirred slightly, trying to distract himself.

Lisa moved but didn't open her eyes. The hand that lay on his chest also moved, with a slow, downward stroke that made David's breath catch in his throat.

'Mmm.' The hand stopped only briefly. The invitation was irresistible.

David bent his head to her breast with a happy groan. The hours of joyous discovery last night had given him the confidence to know that whatever either of them did, it was perfect. It just didn't get any better than this. And Lisa seemed to be in agreement. When the alarm clock sounded, some time later, she ignored it.

'What have you done to me, David James? I'm usually up long before the alarm goes off.'

'Exactly what I've wanted to do to you since the first moment I saw you,' David murmured. 'I still can't believe you've changed your mind.'

'I haven't.'

David's eyes flew open. He propped himself up on one elbow so he could try and gauge Lisa's expression. She was grinning at him.

'I fancied you something rotten as soon as you walked into my office. *Your* office, I mean.'

'You hid it very well.'

'Of course. I've had a lot of practice.'

'You mean, you fancy lots of men something rotten?'

'No!' Lisa gave him a shove. 'I mean I've had a lot of practice not letting personal feelings interfere with my career. Besides, your reputation had preceded you, thanks to Jane and Mike. I was determined to dislike you on sight.'

'That was certainly the impression I got.'

'And then you turned up with that rose just after I'd readmitted Desmond Knight and got myself really steamed up about cardiac surgeons in general and Lewis Tanner in particular.'

'You let me have it with both barrels,' David agreed solemnly. 'You were scary—but I still fancied you.'

'And then…*then* you made that crack about library books and I knew you were just the same as all the rest.'

'It was a joke,' David protested. 'Not one that I'd have mentioned if I'd known a woman was present. And I don't personally subscribe to the philosophy.' Not any more, anyway, he added silently. God, he wanted to tell her that he loved her and could never want anyone else ever again. A warning bell rang loudly. Lisa didn't want to hear something that heavy with all its long-term implications.

'What about your famous reputation?' Lisa demanded. 'Listening to Jane Maddon and Mike, it sounded like you'd been on *very* friendly terms with every female in the hospital.'

'I hope so,' David said thoughtfully. 'I might have missed one or two, I guess.'

Lisa gasped and shoved him again.

'I didn't sleep with them all.' David caught Lisa's hand and pinned it to the bed. 'I'm very particular. And what about you? What about Alan Bennett *and* Sean Findlay? Hmm?'

Lisa's jaw dropped. 'They're *friends*. That's *all*!'

'Touché.' David still held Lisa's hand trapped. He bent and kissed her lips. 'Now, where were we?'

'No! We've got to get up. It's Monday.' Lisa wriggled away decisively. 'We have careers waiting for us. Mike and I are on take today.'

'Guess who got admitted this morning?' Lisa bit hungrily into a ham salad bagel at lunchtime.

'Not Harry?'

Lisa nodded and swallowed. 'He asked to be transferred here rather than Dunedin. We've lined him up to have a defibrillator implanted tomorrow morning.'

'I'm not sure I can fit it in.' David frowned. 'You could have asked first.'

'Why should we?' Lisa looked bemused. 'We do it ourselves.'

'It's always been the job of a surgeon where I've been.'

'What's always been the job of a surgeon?' Mike deposited his tray on the table beside them and sat down. 'Being a hero?' He began unloading his tray. 'Did you guys know there's a picture of your bus in this morning's newspaper? Do you have any idea of how close you came to falling off that cliff?' Mike shook his head. 'You should have followed my example and stayed in bed. Both of you.'

David caught Lisa's eye. Mike glanced up from his sandwich in time to catch the lingering look they exchanged. A wide grin spread over his face.

'Like that, is it?' He nodded with evident self-satisfaction. 'I told you you were perfect for each other. Another problem solved, mate.'

'You could say that.' David winked at Lisa. 'Frustration's not a pleasant symptom.'

'I mean about your accommodation.' Mike reached for his coffee.

'What are you talking about, Mike?'

'Dave's getting kicked out of the staff quarters this week. He needs somewhere to live.'

'So?' David winced at Lisa's measured tone.

'So he can move in with you.'

'Hey, wait a minute, mate,' David said forcefully. He wanted to erase the look of alarm he saw in Lisa's face. 'We're not talking walking up the aisle here.'

'Course not. I wouldn't dream of suggesting it to either of you career freaks. But think about it.' Mike picked up his last sandwich. 'With the hours you two work it's the only way you'd get to see each other, let alone— Ouch!' Mike glared at Lisa. 'Kicking your boss under the table is no way to get promotion, Dr Kennedy. And I know you're after my job.'

'She's after my job as well.' David eagerly latched onto the change of subject. 'She wants to put in an implantable defibrillator. That's surgeon stuff in my book.'

'We like to pretend sometimes.' Mike grinned. 'I was actually planning to wield the scalpel myself.' He leaned back in his chair. 'No reason why we can't all come to the party. You can put it in, Dave, and Lisa and I will run the electrophysiology side and do the follow-up testing.'

David looked at Lisa. 'Is that OK with you?'

'Sure. Harry will probably be very reassured.' Lisa's mouth twitched but David leaned forward.

'Any more remarks about *real* doctors and it'll be you that gets kicked under the table. I do happen to have a personal interest in this particular case.'

Mike stood up and collected his empty plate and cup. 'I've got to run. Got an angioplasty due. I'll leave you two to play under the table by yourselves. Have fun.'

'I've got to go too,' David told Lisa reluctantly. 'My outpatient clinic starts in five minutes. Will I see you later?' He lowered his voice. 'I would *really* like to see you later.'

Lisa's colour heightened. 'I'm on take. I don't know when I'll get away.' She hesitated and dropped her gaze. 'I'd like to see you, too.'

There was a longer pause and David knew they were

both thinking of what Mike had suggested. Lisa finally glanced up and smiled tentatively.

'Maybe I'll get lucky. I'll give you a ring if I'm not too busy.'

The call did not eventuate and Lisa looked weary enough the next day for David to believe she hadn't had the chance to make any personal calls. Lisa gave no indication of regret, however.

'Harry's signed the consent form but I think he's having second thoughts. Could you have a word with him and then beep me when, or if, you get up to Theatre? I'm a bit caught up in the unit. We've got a temporary pacing wire to put in one of our overnight customers.'

Harry, the bus driver, was understandably nervous.

'Do you mean you're going to knock me off and then see if you can revive me? I think I might give it a miss after all, Dave. Sounds dicey to me.'

'The risk is one that you're walking around with all the time, Harry. Any sudden shock, or stress, or pain might cause your heart to go into an abnormal rhythm and simply stop. Could be something as simple as a thunderstorm.' David paused and let the memory of Harry's brush with death resurface a little more clearly.

'The device we're planning to put in is this.' David held up a small silver object like an undersized cigarette case.

'Can't fit my smokes in that.' Harry grinned.

'What smokes? You told me you'd given up.'

'I have, I have. Isn't that enough to cure me?'

'It will certainly help, but not with your rhythm abnormality.' David tapped the silver case. 'This has a little wire attached to it that will sit inside your heart. If your heart stops it will deliver a very small electrical charge which will restart it. You might not be lucky enough to have a cardiologist to jump on your chest next time.'

'That's what Lisa said. Boy, I wish I'd been awake when she was giving me the kiss of life.' Harry looked wistful but then saw David's frown and grinned. 'How do you know it's going to work?'

'We test it.' David patiently went back to repeat the beginning of the interview. 'We use a stronger electrical current to put you heart into its abnormal rhythm and then we wait to see if this implantable defibrillator does its job and starts your heart up again.'

Harry swallowed hard. 'And if it doesn't?'

'Then we have all the equipment necessary to do it ourselves. Certainly there's a small risk but it isn't nearly as big as the risk you're living with all the time.'

'I'll be asleep, right?'

'Right. You won't know about any of it.'

'Well, that's OK, then.'

It was a relatively minor surgical procedure. David made the incision just below Harry's collarbone, opening up a pouch beneath the skin for the defibrillator. He located the subclavian vein and inserted the wire.

'Let's light him up,' he suggested.

Lisa pulled the handle on the overhead X-ray equipment and eased it over Harry's chest. David depressed the foot pedal to start imaging and they all stared at the screen. Lisa manoeuvred the machine into a better position.

'It's in the liver,' she announced.

David gently pulled the wire back, still watching the screen. 'That looks pretty good.' He placed a stay suture on the end of the wire and Mike clipped it onto the dummy defibrillator unit.

'Let's induce ventricular fibrillation. Give him fifty hertz, Lisa.'

'We'll try two shocks,' David added. 'If the second one doesn't revert then rescue us with the external paddles, please, Lisa.'

'OK.' Lisa adjusted a knob on the machine beside her. 'Delivering fifty hertz now. We've got VF. Cardiac arrest!'

Mike was holding the tiny defibrillator. 'Device sensing... Charging...' There was a click like a light switch being flicked off. Harry's hands jerked once. 'Successful reversion with twenty-four joules,' Mike announced.

David got Harry's defibrillator off the sterile trolley and slipped it into the pouch he'd created. They tested again and got a successful result with a minimal sixteen-joule charge. Satisfied, David closed the wound. 'When are you going to do the retest?'

'Friday morning. We'll just use the treatment room on the ward. IV sedation rather than a full anaesthetic. Feel free to join us if you've got the time.'

David caught Lisa's eye as she was leaving the theatre. 'Are you free tonight?'

'I'm going to have to crash after last night. I wouldn't be great company. How about tomorrow?'

'*I'm* on call.' David smiled ruefully. 'But maybe we'll get lucky.'

They didn't. David dialed 1 for an outside line at 8 p.m.

'Lisa, I'm sorry, I can't get away. We've got a three-year-old boy who's inhaled a piece of balloon. We're about to take him up to Theatre. I'll be too late by the time we've finished.'

By Thursday David was seriously frustrated. His

night with Lisa was beginning to take on a dreamlike quality. A taste of nirvana that might never be repeated. For the first time in his working life he began to wonder at the wisdom of a career choice that interfered so blatantly with a personal life. Lisa seemed to be taking the delay calmly. By Friday David was not only frustrated, he was worried. The more time went by the more opportunity Lisa had to change her mind about seeing him again. Dropping some papers into his office mid-afternoon, David saw Lisa disappearing into her own office. He strode after her, shut the door of her office behind him and stood with his back firmly against it, glowering.

'This is driving me crazy, Lisa. Why can't we find any time to be together?' The treadmill started up in the adjacent exercise testing laboratory and David groaned. 'Now we can't even have a conversation without a 747 taking off next door.'

Lisa stepped closer to David and any worries he might have had concerning her possible reluctance to see him again evaporated as he saw his own frustration mirrored in her intense gaze. He reached out and touched her lips, astonished at Lisa's instant response as she closed her eyes. Her faint moan undid him completely. If he had to beg then so be it.

'Tonight,' he urged. 'Please!'

Lisa jerked her head unhappily. 'I can't. Mike and I are going down to Timaru. There's a dinner meeting of local doctors and GPs. We're showing them some angiography and angioplasty films. We agreed to it months ago.' She bit her lip and looked away from David. 'And I'm on call again this weekend.'

David's groan was almost loud enough to be heard over the roar of the treadmill. Whoever was being tested didn't seem to be suffering from overly severe exertional angina. As though in response to his thought, the treadmill came to a sudden halt.

Lisa was still chewing her lip as she raised her eyes tentatively to meet David's.

'Have you found somewhere else to live yet, David?'

David shook his head and snorted with unamused laughter. 'If I can't find time to see you, why on earth would I make time to do something I don't even want to do?'

'Maybe Mike had a point,' Lisa said quietly. 'Living together might be the only way to see each other. I've got a spare bedroom at my place.'

David couldn't suppress his incredulous chuckle. 'Do you really expect me to live in the same house as you and occupy a separate bedroom, Lisa?'

Her eyes dropped as the colour flooded her cheeks. 'No. It's just that…it's not something I've ever done before. I…I wouldn't want you to get the wrong idea, David.'

'I'm not.' David touched a finger gently under Lisa's chin which had the desired effect of bringing her gaze back up to his. He knew what this was about. Lisa was taking a step towards trusting him. A big step. 'I know what you want, Lisa. And I know what you *don't* want. I feel the same.' His voice caught. 'Trust me.'

She was still struggling. 'What about…the others?'

'The others?'

'Yes. Like the echo technician, Jenny. And what's-her-name—Melanie.'

David would have laughed except that the horrifying implications of his deception flashed through his mind. He could have told her of his relationship to Melanie when the subject had first arisen. But he hadn't. He hadn't forgotten the wave of pleasure it had given him to discover that Lisa was jealous of another woman in his life. The deception had been deliberate.

And now he was begging her to trust him. The moment was too crucial to jeopardise. Lisa's gaze was searching and there was a hint of desperation in their dark depths. She wanted to trust him but she had been let down by too many men in her life. This was a huge risk she was considering. If he let her down now, even in a small way, he would lose. And David had no intention of losing.

'There's no one else in my life, Lisa. Only you.'

She couldn't doubt his sincerity. He was telling the truth after all.

'That's all right, then.' Lisa's gaze relaxed and she broke the intense eye contact. 'We may as well give it a go, I guess. I wouldn't like to see you put out onto the streets.' She glanced back, her confidence returning. 'Can you cook?'

'Of course.' David grinned and straightened as his beeper sounded. 'Can you?'

Lisa's eyes narrowed speculatively. 'We'll see. I'll organise a key for you, then. If I'm home you can cook tomorrow night.'

It was Lisa's turn to visit David's office after her ward round on Saturday morning. 'I've brought you a key. I'm not sure when I'll get home.'

'Are you sure about this, Lisa?' David asked gently. 'I'll understand if you've changed your mind.'

'You mean about it being your turn to cook?' Lisa's gaze was wary. 'Of course I haven't changed my mind. You won't get off that easily.'

'That wasn't quite what I meant,' David muttered.

'Here's your key.' Lisa produced the item from her

white coat pocket. Her fingers shook a little as she held it out and David knew she was nervous about the risk she was taking.

The thought aroused a protective instinct in him that he found strangely satisfying. He closed his hand around hers to steady it. 'Don't worry.' He smiled re-assuringly. 'I'm a great cook…really!'

The Wednesday morning coronary artery bypass case was a marathon. Five grafts and three attempts to wean off bypass meant that it was well past lunchtime when they finished, but David felt great.

The last few nights had been just as good as the first they'd had together. Better, even, because now his shirts hung in the wardrobe beside Lisa's clothes. His tooth-brush stood beside hers on the bathroom shelf.

'Make sure you put the top back on the tube,' Lisa had told him sternly that morning. 'I can't stand oozy toothpaste.'

'Come in the shower with me, Lisa.' David poked his head around the curtain and grinned. 'I fancy rub-bing soapy hands all over that glorious body of yours.'

Lisa hesitated. 'You're on call tonight, aren't you?'

'Sure am,' David called. He could see Lisa's outline through the curtain as she slowly untied the knot on her dressing-gown cord. 'Don't know when—or if—I'll make it home.' He reached for the soap as the curtain twitched back. He hadn't expected Lisa to disrupt her getting-ready-for-work routine and respond to his invi-tation, but her unpredictability was one of the things he loved about her. Awkward when she wanted to pick a fight but incredibly arousing when she chose to respond physically. He was never quite sure which way she would jump. Life was an exciting business these days.

David's feeling of well-being carried him through a heavy week of duties, including a gruelling respiratory outpatient clinic on Thursday afternoon. A downturn in his mood only occurred when his last patient came through the door. The man was seventy-four, his breathing sounded laboured and his wife looked frightened. David knew that neither of them would leave the appointment feeling reassured.

'I have all the reports that came from your GP, Mr Parkinson, and the test results from your appointments with the respiratory physicians. Did Dr Wallace discuss the results of your bronchoscopy with you?' David had been caught in Theatre but his senior registrar had coped well with the procedure.

His patient nodded. 'Kind of.'

David returned the nod. The shock of the initial confirmation of a malignancy often rendered patients incapable of retaining much of the information they received. 'You have a cancerous growth on the left side of the main part of the airway to your left lung.' David indicated the area on the X-ray illuminated on the wall viewing screen. 'Are you a smoker, Mr Parkinson?'

'Yes.'

'How long for?'

'About sixty years. My father was a heavy smoker,' he added, as though excusing himself.

'And what happened to him?'

'Lung cancer.'

Mrs Parkinson clicked open her handbag and removed a handkerchief, which she pressed against her eyes. David's spirits sank a little further.

'Your lung-function tests show us that your respiratory system isn't in great shape.' David took a deep breath. 'That makes surgery a significant risk, especially if we remove the whole lung. What we need to do now is weigh up the risks so that you can make a decision.'

Mr Parkinson nodded slowly.

'The long-term risk is obviously the cancer. The short-term risk is the surgery. You have maybe a one to two per cent chance of not making it through the operation or getting out of hospital.'

'Lewis wouldn't touch him.'

'I don't suppose he would. His statistics must be wonderful.'

'The best.' Lisa nestled her head against David's shoulder and curled her feet up on the couch. The television was just a background mumble, a late night news broadcast neither of them were following.

'He doesn't have the right to refuse treatment because of his judgement of people,' David said angrily.

'He thinks he does. Of course, he finds good medical reasons for refusal.'

'God complex,' David muttered. 'I hate that.'

'Me too.'

'Addiction is an illness in itself,' David continued quietly. 'We can try to treat it but if we can't then we need to try and treat the consequences. Just as we would if the patient were hypertensive or diabetic.'

'That reminds me. We readmitted Serafina Judd to-day. Her angina's worse and she's come in under Lewis's name. Next week's meeting should be fun.'

David's jaw had sagged. 'I don't *believe* it!'

'Just wait.' Lisa's head popped up. 'He thinks obesity is just as much of a personal failing as smoking. He'll wriggle out of any—'

David was grinning broadly as he interrupted Lisa. '*What* did you say her name was?'

'Serafina.'

David laughed. 'I love it! Makes you think of cherubs...or fairies.'

Lisa laughed too. 'She has lost ten kilos in the last three weeks but she's nowhere near flying yet.'

David stared down into Lisa's laughing brown eyes. His own smile faded as his emotions focused. The sound of her laughter and the sparkle in the depths of her eyes captured his heart. Her happiness was more important than his own. Far more important. Lisa's face stilled as she registered his intensity. The look they held wasn't broken by any words and its ending was inevitable. David could convey what he felt with his lips and hands far more eloquently than he could phrase it verbally. And Lisa seemed willing to accept the physical expression.

No mention was made out loud of any emotional depth. It seemed to David to have been a ground rule right from the start, and it had been confirmed as the days sped past. He had no desire to break any rules that made this possible. If this was as good as it was going to get then that was more than enough for him.

Mike *had* been right. Their time together was precious. On Sunday they had the rare treat of an entire day without any medical commitments. The spring weather was perfect and Lisa suggested a ride in her car with the roof down. They roared off out of town, taking the road to the Bank's Peninsula, and Lisa whooped with joy when they reached the twisting hillside road after a long stretch of straight driving.

'Now you'll see what she can *really* do!' Lisa yelled.

David's fingers tightened on the leather upholstery but by the time they reached the bottom of the enor-

mous hill he, too, was shouting gleefully as they accel-
erated out of each corner.

The exhilaration faded into a contented companion-
ship when they reached the small and originally French
settlement of Akaroa. They walked through the town-
ship, admiring the quaint cottages and French road
signs. They sipped cappuccinos at an outdoor café and
watched the activity of yachts on the picture-postcard
harbour.

'Let's stay the night,' David said suddenly.

'We haven't brought any clothes!'

'So? Who needs clothes?' David hooded his eyes and
was gratified to hear Lisa's sharp intake of breath.

'I was thinking about work. It's Monday tomorrow.'

'We can leave early enough to get home and change.
Forget work. Some things are more important. Like us.'

It had been a perfect evening. Even leaving at 5.30 a.m.
to make it back to Christchurch in time to change and
get to the hospital by 7.30 a.m. had been worth it. It
was a treat unlikely to be repeated in the near future.
More often than not during the week, any time together
was interrupted. As it was on Tuesday evening.

'I'm sorry I'm so late. We had an emergency. A
woman was stabbed by her de facto husband.'

'I thought Lewis was on call.'

'He was. He was also halfway through surgery on
someone at Greenpark. Someone had to fill in or the
woman would have died.'

'Is she OK?'

'She will be. We'll be keeping her in Intensive Care
for a few days, though. I may have to go back in later
tonight. Have you eaten?'

'I had the leftover pizza.' Lisa screwed up her nose in distaste. 'I thought you said you could cook.'

'I can,' David insisted. 'When I have the time.' Luckily he was unlikely to have to prove it, the way things were going.

'That remains to be seen,' Lisa pronounced. 'All you've provided so far have been take-aways. You must have the number of every restaurant in town that delivers.'

'Yeah.' David's grin was unrepentant. 'I hope so.'

'You're not on tomorrow, are you?'

'No.'

'Neither am I.'

'Let's toss a coin. See who gets to do the honours.'

'It's your turn.'

'Why?' David tried to look offended. 'I haven't experienced the delights of your culinary skills yet.'

'What? I made an omelette. Last week.'

'Was that what it was?' David checked that Lisa's hands were empty of any potential missiles. 'I thought it was an edible paper plate. Aren't omelettes supposed to be, you know...fluffy?'

'I never said *I* could cook. You said *you* could cook. Why do you think I invited you to move in?'

'I know exactly why.' David moved closer. 'You fancied me something rotten. You only wanted my body.'

'Mmm.' Lisa also stepped closer. 'That's right. How could I have forgotten?'

The touch of their lips was enough to dispel any other thoughts. It could even dispel David's alarming impression that Lisa wasn't joking. That all she wanted from him was their physical relationship. They shared an addiction to each other's bodies. Was that all that was holding them together?

David arrived early at the hospital the following morning, thanks to a lift in Lisa's little red car.

'You'd better get rid of that heap of rust,' she advised David. 'It doesn't do anything for my image, being parked in front of my town house.'

Her image. *Her* town house. David felt shut out. 'I can't afford a new car just yet. Why do you think I moved in? I need a resident mechanic.' He watched Lisa's face closely, hoping for a reaction, but Lisa just smiled.

'Oh, sure!' Her glance reminded him of last night's session. They had been almost naked by the time they were halfway to the bedroom. And that had only been the beginning! Her expression was thoughtful as she swiped her pass card through the slot that controlled the barrier arm into the staff car park. 'Why don't you have any money, David?'

'I give it away,' David said ruefully. He thought of the cheque he had posted to Melanie yesterday. It was going to be the last one. It was more than time his sister learned to cope by herself. Perhaps she'd better marry the opal miner—and soon—but the tone of her letter had been worrying. She was planning to head home again, it seemed. Alone. David shook off the worry that trouble was looming. 'Would you rather I were rich, Lisa? Maybe I can go into hock on a BMW or something.'

Lisa switched off her car's engine. 'No.' She gave David a rather shy smile. 'I like the fact that you don't seem to care about money. It was when I found you with that broken-down heap, holding up the traffic, that I thought maybe I'd been wrong about you after all. You *weren't* like all the others.'

'I won't be poor for ever.' David reached into the

back seat to collect his briefcase. 'I had some debts to repay, but I've done that now.'

'Debts?' Lisa raised her eyebrows. 'Is this where I get to hear about the ex-wife or the gambling addiction?'

David laughed. 'My parents went through a lot, paying for my education. I bought them a house last year.'

'Really?' Lisa's eyes widened. 'Not many people would do that.'

'Not many people have such great parents.' David hesitated. 'I'd love you to meet them, Lisa. Why don't you come up to Auckland with me for a weekend?' David knew he'd said the wrong thing as soon as the words left his lips. Lisa's eyes looked like shutters had gone up.

'Pass,' she said lightly. She opened her door and David followed suit.

'Why not?' He had been encouraged by her comments about his finances. Now he was being shut out again and he didn't like it.

'What would your parents think? About us living together, I mean?'

'They'd think that I'd finally found the perfect woman. They'd be thrilled.'

'Exactly. And then what would they think?'

David strode out to keep pace with Lisa. He stayed silent. He couldn't admit that, of course, they would expect news of an engagement or marriage plans. The silence continued and deepened. David struggled with an urge to tell Lisa that he loved her. What was so wrong with the idea of marriage anyway? He was getting quite used to the idea. Maybe Lisa might, too. Perhaps it just needed the right words to sow the seed. But David had no idea what those words might be.

'Let's just leave our families out of this,' Lisa suggested firmly as they reached the main entrance. 'We don't need the complications.'

'Kiss,' David murmured.

'In the main foyer? In your dreams, mate!'

'No.' David grinned. 'Kiss as in, "Keep it simple, stupid". Our relationship,' he added. 'No complications.'

Lisa nodded, but her eyes were on her watch. 'Kiss, it is, then. Have a good day, David.'

David detoured into the cardiology ward on his way to his office. He checked the names on the doors and entered Room 4 as the breakfast trolley was being loaded for removal.

'Mrs Judd?'

'Hello, dear. How nice to see you. How's your baby?' Mrs Judd was in bed, attached to the IV infusion that was controlling her angina.

'It wasn't my baby,' David reminded her. He pulled out a chair and sat down. 'But I do need some more advice. What do you know about making omelettes, Mrs Judd?'

'Call me Serafina, dear. Everybody does. Omelettes, you said?'

'Mmm.' David leaned closer. 'Really fluffy ones.'

CHAPTER NINE

LEWIS TANNER'S abrupt resignation from the cardi-othoracic surgical team at Christchurch Hospital the following week was a shock but no great surprise.

'It was all your doing, you know,' Lisa admonished David. They were in bed, a now-familiar haven. Passion had been sated, at least temporarily, but neither of them felt inclined to sleep.

'What was? Seems to me you were quite an active partner.' David stroked his hand down Lisa's arm, brushed suggestively over her breast and finally caught hold of her hand.

'I'm talking about Lewis resigning. You were the straw that broke the camel's back.'

'Was I?' David sounded pleased. 'How do you make that out?'

'Well, there he was in the meeting last week, offering every reason he could think of why he couldn't operate on Mrs Judd, and you look up with that innocent expression and say, "But, Lewis—she doesn't *smoke*!" ' Lisa gurgled with laughter. 'I thought he was going to walk out then and there.'

'I think the resignation had more to do with Alan laying down the law and saying that refusal to operate due to personal preferences was unacceptable.'

'And the fact that he'd been operating at Greenpark the night he was on call here and that stabbing victim came in. Even management was disgusted over that one.'

'All's well that ends well, I guess. Apart from the extra workload that Alan and I will have to shoulder until we get a replacement.' It was David's turn to chuckle. 'Who would have guessed that Serafina Judd would end up being patient number one in our trial?'

'How's she doing tonight?'

'Great. We had a long talk—about omelettes.'

'What?' Lisa propped herself up on her elbow.

'I have to confess. You remember that omelette I made that night?'

'The one night you actually did some genuine cooking? How could I forget? It was great.'

'It was, wasn't it? Really fluffy.' David sighed. 'It was Mrs Judd who told me how to do it.' His voice rose in a fair imitation of their shared patient. 'Beat the yolks and whites separately, dear. Half a tablespoon of water to each yolk and make sure you beat the whites till you've got firm peaks. Then fold them together— very gently. Don't let the air escape—'

Lisa was laughing helplessly. 'You fraud! And I thought you could really cook.'

'I can. Omelettes!'

'You'd better expand your repertoire. I've invited Mike and Anne to dinner next week. I found a night when none of us are on call.'

'Oh, no! Can't we have pizza?'

'No way. I'm bored stiff with take-aways.'

'You cook, then.'

'Pass.' Lisa was grinning wickedly. 'I fix cars. I don't *do* dinners.'

'Why on earth did you invite dinner guests, then? This is *your* problem, Lisa. Don't expect me to bail you out. Omelettes are it.'

'I invited them for you, David. Mike was making

forlorn noises about never seeing you any more. He suggested that I was monopolising your company.'

'I'm not complaining.' David bent his head to kiss her. 'Monopolise me some more.'

'Mmm.' Lisa's arms came up willingly to allow David to move in closer. 'But I can't cancel Mike. He said he can't wait to taste your cooking.'

'I'll bet,' David said grimly. 'He knows I can't cook.' He began raining small kisses over Lisa's face.

'Let's compromise,' he suggested persuasively. 'I'll do the main course. You do dessert. Think of it as a research project. A collaboration—as equal partners.' He raised his head. 'We're good at that, aren't we?'

'Oh, yes.' Lisa pulled David's head down, her lips parted expectantly. 'We're very good at collaborating.'

It was nearly a month now since David had moved in with Lisa. What had seemed perfect to begin with was now seeming more and more like a shell. Something was missing and David knew exactly what it was. It was what Lisa didn't want. Commitment. Something more. It was easy to let it slide. Their arguments were minor and even when they weren't they both enjoyed the making up that followed swiftly. It was their physical relationship that was the glue holding them together and it increasingly bothered David that this was the case.

He hadn't pushed—yet. He hadn't even told Lisa that he loved her, although on several occasions he had almost bitten his tongue to prevent the words escaping. Instead, he tried to convey how he felt in bed and her response was always all he could ask for. Except that now it wasn't. He wanted to ask for more. And he was afraid she would refuse.

They had enrolled their fourth patient in their Neuroshield trial now. Lisa was talking about setting up a statistical programme to start entering the data for later analysis. She was right. They were good at collaborating. They spent a lot of time discussing the overlap of their caseload.

Serafina Judd was due for discharge by the end of the week. They had both been delighted by her uneventful recovery from surgery. If anyone had noticed David sitting beside her bed, making rapid notes, they wouldn't have thought it particularly unusual. Had they come close enough to hear the conversation they might well have changed their minds.

'Sear the meat at a high temperature first, dear. Then turn it down to cook slowly. Put your vegetables in the pan an hour and a half before you plan to serve dinner. I always like a roast for a dinner party. It gives you plenty of time to talk to your guests.'

'And I get to carve.' David grinned. 'I should be good at that at least.'

Desmond Knight had been seen in David's outpatient clinic but he provided the basis for his conversation with Lisa over supper that night.

'He's complaining of sternal pain. It's enough to make sleeping difficult and he's frustrated because it's interfering with his rehabilitation programme.'

'Non-union of the sternum, do you think?' Lisa looked concerned.

'I've booked a CT scan but I don't think so. It's quite stable clinically. I couldn't find any evidence of a click. The upper part of the sternal wound is very tender, though.'

'It's a bit early for new bone formation to show up on CT, isn't it?'

David nodded. 'And the edges are often distorted by the chest retractors so they won't line up perfectly anyway. It can give a false impression of non-union.'

'Maybe he's sensitive to the sternal wires.'

'Could be. I've started him on a non-steroidal anti-inflammatory.'

'Can you take the wires out?'

'Yes, but not until there's been enough time for a good union. I'd leave it a few months yet. I'm going to see him again next week, after the scan.'

Harry, the bus driver, had been seen by Lisa in Mike's outpatient clinic. David was pleased to hear about his clearance to return home.

'He's a bit disappointed to have to give up the driving,' Lisa reported, 'but he's happy he has less chance of dropping dead unexpectedly.'

'What's he going to do?'

'Apparently he's lined up a job with the bungee jumping outfit. He said something like, "I can't wait to push those suckers off the bridge."'

'Sounds like Harry. Let's hope he doesn't try it himself. I'm not sure his defibrillator would cope with that.'

Stephen Taylor was very much a shared patient. He would be in hospital for at least two months before they could be confident he was fit for release. He was now in his sixth week following the surgery and so far he had been doing brilliantly. The day before Mike and Anne were due to come for dinner, however, Lisa beeped David.

They met outside Stephen's private room. Lisa was still wearing the gown, hat and mask she had worn to enter the room due to the reverse isolation protection that Stephen still needed. The mask was pushed down to hang around Lisa's neck and she was holding a sheet of biochemical test requisition forms.

'It's nothing I can put my finger on,' she told David anxiously. 'I just know something's not right. He hasn't been doing any schoolwork all day or even listening to music. I brought him in the latest copy of *Classic Car* and he wasn't really interested. Said he might read it tomorrow.'

'Signs?'

'Temperature's up but only slightly. BP's fine. Heart rate's 105 but 95 to 100 is normal for a denervated heart. He says he feels a bit ''blah''.'

David smiled. 'I know about ''blah''. We had a special lecture at medical school.'

'It could be anything from the start of a cold to rejection.' Lisa waved the forms she held. 'I may be overreacting.'

'What have you lined up?'

'Blood count, chest X-ray, echo, blood and urine cultures and a throat swab.'

'Biopsy?'

'Of course—first thing tomorrow, but I'm wondering if I should try and call the cath lab staff in and get it done tonight. I thought I'd talk to you and then we could both talk to Mike.'

'Have you checked the cyclosporine levels?'

'It's on the list. Stephen's not going to be too impressed by the amount of blood I'm going to take off.'

'I'll come in and distract him.' David pulled a hat and mask from the dispensing boxes attached to the wall. 'Grab me some of those cute little bootees, could you, please, Lisa?'

The biopsy was done later that evening. Stephen's temperature and heart rate had increased by the time Mike joined them, and he was complaining of chest pain. Nobody wanted to take any chances on a possible episode of rejection. Mike did the biopsy, feeding a catheter through the subclavian vein to bite tiny samples of tissue from the ventricle of Stephen's new heart. Microscopic examination would confirm any inflammatory reaction that indicated an attempt by Stephen's immune system to destroy the foreign tissue.

The results would be some hours away, however, and David and Lisa decided to go ahead with their planned shopping expedition for dinner-party supplies as the supermarket was one that stayed open until midnight. Lisa rang the hospital as soon as they got home but no results were available yet, apart from the white cell count which was normal.

'Probably not an infection, then.' David nodded. 'And there's no evidence of heart failure so even it if is rejection it's not severe. We'll get on top of it.'

'You bet.' Lisa eyed the items David was unpacking from the carrier bags. 'Do you really know how to cook a leg of lamb?'

'It'll be even better than the omelette,' David promised. 'And *I'm* not going to cheat. You agreed to make dessert, remember?'

'I am. See?'

David glanced at the large cardboard box. 'Buying a ready-made pavlova doesn't count.'

'But I'm going to whip the cream and do something pretty with kiwifruit. We can pretend I made it.'

'Pretending doesn't work.' David put down the pumpkin he was holding, suddenly serious. 'You tend to get found out and someone winds up hurt—or em-

barrassed.' Now that he had started, David was unable
to stop his next words. 'Like pretending we're living
together.'

'We *are* living together.'

'In your house. You won't even let me pay rent, Lisa.
I feel like a guest.'

'You bought all these groceries...and you've spent a
fortune on take-aways in the last month.'

'OK. I feel like a caterer, then. Like an extra. Like
I'm not really a part of your life.' David knew he was
stepping onto dangerous ground. He didn't need to see
the wariness in Lisa's face to know that he was breaking
the rules.

'You're more a part of my life than anyone else has
been.' Lisa seemed fascinated by the kiwifruit she was
holding. 'We're living together. Isn't that enough for
you?'

'Depends on your definition of living, doesn't it,
Lisa? Are you trying to make sure I don't get too far
in? Does it make you feel more in control of the situation if I'm just a visitor?'

'If I had been in control you wouldn't be here at all.'
The admission seemed ripped from her.

There was a moment of shocked silence before David
spoke very quietly. 'Do you want me to leave? Is that
what you want?'

'What do *you* want, David?'

'I want...' David felt his face contort with the effort
of trying to formulate the right words. Or, rather, trying
not to say what sprang instantly to mind. He wanted to
say, I love you, Lisa. I want to hear you say that *you*
love me. What then? She might say, ''But I don't love
you. There's no room in my life for that kind of com-

mitment. You *know* that.''' He did know it. And he wasn't prepared to precipitate a final showdown.

'I want what you want, Lisa,' he said heavily. '*Do* you want me to leave?'

She seemed to be having the same struggle he had just had. The silence seemed interminable. David's future was hanging in the balance. He felt like he was playing Russian roulette. Was the bullet coming in this shot?

'No,' she whispered finally, unable to meet David's eyes. 'I don't want you to leave.'

'Good.' David's voice was raw. 'Because I sure as hell don't *want* to leave.'

The space was still there between them. The tension still high. David recognised the opportunity to step into that empty space, to reveal even a little of how he felt— of how much he wanted to stay. The shrill call of the telephone was so intrusive it was painful.

'OK, so it looks like a mild rejection?' He listened wearily as Lisa spoke. 'Can you put me through to the lab? I want to know what the cyclosporine levels are like.'

It was safe ground to retreat to, discussing the plan to deal with Stephen's rejection of his donor heart. It was only mild. They could adjust the immune suppression therapy. Bump up the steroid dose and maybe start a high-dose IV steroid if control proved difficult.

The knowledge of their shared admission of wanting to stay together hung between them but nothing more was said. David could sense the new dimension in their love-making that night. It was a confirmation of their need to be together. A recognition that while the future might be too complicated to consider, their need to be together was too great to contemplate a termination.

Next day Stephen still showed no signs of any heart failure, which would have indicated a worsening of his condition and necessitate intensive monitoring. Both David and Lisa left work earlier than usual and David took over the kitchen the moment they got home.

'Go away,' he ordered Lisa. 'I've got a serious operation to perform in here. I need to concentrate.'

'But I need to make dessert.'

'Ha!' David scoffed. 'Five minutes to whip some cream, that's all you need. I'm the one making the real effort here.' He ushered her back towards the door. 'You go and find some wine. Get some beer as well. I forgot.'

He shook his head as he opened the notebook in which he had scribbled down Mrs Judd's pearls of culinary wisdom. Not so long ago the beer would have been at the top of his list for entertainment requirements. Hell, it would probably have been the only thing on the list. Times had changed.

Lisa took so long to return that David thought their guests might arrive first. She tried in vain to find a clear space to set the bottles down in the kitchen.

'My God, David. It looks like a bomb's gone off.'

'Ah!' David followed her stunned appraisal of the room. 'You should have stayed after all, Lisa. I think I needed a scrub nurse.'

'You sure need one now. What's that all over the walls?'

'Potato peelings. Haven't you seen any before?'

'Not stuck to the walls.' Lisa's smile was disbelieving. 'You must have been rather enthusiastic.' She sniffed cautiously. 'Doesn't smell too bad, though.'

'It's going to be perfect. You can do your dessert now.' David offered. 'I'm going to get changed.'

Lisa gazed around again. 'Just where am I supposed to do that? In the bathroom?'

'You can if you like but I'm planning to have a shower. Your pav might get a bit soggy.'

The doorbell rang as David emerged ten minutes later. Mike was carrying a six pack. Anne was carrying the baby. Lisa's eyes met David's with dismay. Mike caught the glance.

'Sorry, we had to bring Sophie. Our babysitter got sick and Anne's mum isn't up to doing the honours again just yet.'

'She won't be any trouble,' promised Anne.

Sophie took one look at David and burst into tears.

'He has this way with women,' Lisa said, laughing.

Anne looked worried. She jiggled the baby reassuringly and then smiled brightly. 'Something smells wonderful! What is it?'

'That's David's department.' Lisa was glaring at Sophie as though a stern look would be enough to turn off the tears. David's heart sank. She really wasn't into kids at all. But, then, neither was he so why should the confirmation make him feel disappointed?

Mike handed David the beer. 'This I've got to see. When did you learn to cook, mate?' He began to follow David into the kitchen.

'It's a fairly recent accomplishment,' David said modestly. Mike appeared not to have heard.

'Good grief, man! What have you been *doing* in here?'

'Cooking,' David said firmly. He began to steer Mike out of the door again. 'Come through here. I'll get you a beer.'

Mike had caught sight of the dessert, perched precariously between a spilled bag of flour and the debris

from the dismembered pumpkin. He whistled appreciatively. '*Mate!* I take it all back. You must be some kind
of genius!'

'Lisa made the dessert.' David caught Lisa's eye and
grinned as she blushed. She opened her mouth, obviously on the point of confessing, then she snapped it
shut and returned David's grin. He winked, enjoying the
collusion.

Sophie was now sitting on a rug on the floor, banging
two wooden blocks together.

'We brought the port-a-cot,' Mike announced. 'She'll
crash soon.'

David handed Mike a beer and put a bowl of crisps
on the coffee-table. Sophie dropped her blocks and held
out a small hand commandingly. David smiled at Anne.

'A lady who knows what she wants. I like that. Is
she allowed one?'

Anne nodded indulgently and David selected a large
crisp and offered it to Sophie. She accepted and ex-
amined the offering with rapt attention, before putting
it into her mouth. Then she withdrew it and offered it
back to David, bestowing a beaming smile on him.

'That's OK,' David said hurriedly. 'You keep it,
Soph.' He bit back a smile. 'Quite cute, isn't she?'

'Uh-oh!' Mike's tone was ominous. 'He's getting
clucky. Watch out, Lisa.'

There was a moment's awkward silence which David
broke with a laugh, just a fraction too late.

'No chance. Kids aren't on the agenda, are they,
Lisa?' He glanced away from Sophie who was now
moving towards him at a fast crawl.

She was staring at him with a peculiar look of dismay
on her face. David groaned inwardly. He'd put his foot
in it again somehow and he'd only been trying to re-

assure her. Sophie reached the coffee-table. She put her hand on the rim of the crisp bowl as she heaved herself to her feet. The decisive tipping movement of the bowl sent the crisps flying in an arc to cover a wide area of carpet.

'Oh, no!' Anne leapt to her feet. 'Sophie!' She started to pick up the crisps. 'We shouldn't have brought her, Mike. Look at this mess!'

'Don't worry.' Mike popped the tab on his beer can. 'You should see the kitchen!'

'Hadn't you better check on the roast, David?' Lisa's query sent David moving at a fast pace. He had managed to forget his responsibility for the meal since their guests had arrived. God, it might have burnt by now.

He needn't have worried. The meat was cooked to perfection, the roast vegetables crispy, the boiled ones just tender. David was not going to confess that the gravy had come out of a packet and Lisa wouldn't dare say anything, with that pavlova lurking in the kitchen. David's surgical skills were the butt of more than a few jokes as he carved the roast.

'It's not as easy as it looks,' he complained.

'Watch out,' Mike hooted. 'You just severed the pulmonary artery there, mate.'

There were no complaints as they ate. Even Lisa made impressed noises and David basked in the glow of a new achievement. Sophie occupied herself happily, finding crisp fragments in the carpet and eating them, periodically crowing with delight as she found a larger piece. David found his gaze straying to the child more than once.

What would it be like, having a child of your own? What would it be like to have one that was his and Lisa's? David tried to concentrate on his minted peas.

It would probably be a monster. Stubborn, argumentative, challenging, passionate and more often than not—a sheer joy.

'Sorry?' David realised he had missed Mike's comment.

'I just asked how Melanie was these days.'

'Running full tilt towards her next crisis, I expect. As usual.'

Lisa's fork stopped halfway to her mouth. David watched her toy with the contents of her plate for a few seconds before the cause of her sudden loss of appetite occurred to him. Thanks to her rule about not involving their families, he had never got around to explaining that Melanie was his sister. Not that it excused his earlier avoidance of the subject but surely it had been reasonable to want to establish a basis of trust so that the deception could then be seen as an amusing tactic. David tried to look amused now. He made a good attempt at a casual laugh.

'I keep hoping Mel will get married and become someone else's problem.'

'No chance, mate. You'll never get rid of Melanie that easily.' Mike was helping himself to another roasted potato.

David cringed inwardly, desperate to change the subject. If he couldn't catch Lisa alone in the kitchen for a second or two then he'd have to make sure he cleared up her misunderstanding the moment their guests headed home.

'Where is she at the moment?'

'Australia.' David ground out the word and glared at Mike, trying to signal an end to the topic. 'More vegetables, Anne?'

'Thanks. They're wonderful. I must say I've never

thought of you as a domesticated type, David. I'm really impressed.'

Lisa had started eating again and David allowed himself to relax. 'I do a great omelette, too,' he informed Anne. 'And I clean.'

Lisa was inspired to rejoin the conversation. 'He does, too.' She nodded at Anne. 'He cleaned the toilet last week.'

Anne pointed her fork at Mike. 'That's one thing you've never done, Michael Foster. Take note!'

Lisa laughed. 'Be careful. David used the dishwashing brush.'

David didn't join in the explosion of mirth. 'How was I to know?' he protested. 'It was in the cupboard with all the cleaning stuff.'

Mike was still laughing. 'Thank God for that. I was beginning to think you were setting some standard that no husband could ever live up to.'

'I'm not a husband,' David protested. 'Lisa and I are collaborators. Equal partners.'

Lisa nodded. 'Marriage isn't on the agenda. Is it, David?'

David was unsure whether it had been a statement or a question. He met her glance and smiled, he hoped, reassuringly. 'We operate on the Kiss principle,' he explained to Mike.

Mike's eyebrows wriggled. 'I'll just bet you do.'

Lisa blushed. 'He means keeping it simple.'

'Stupid,' added David with a grin.

'No complications,' continued Lisa. 'Like titles or roles. Or expectations. From us—or anyone else. Isn't that right, David?'

'You're the boss,' he said lightly. He met her gaze squarely. It had sounded disturbingly like a warning.

'I thought you were equal partners.' Mike didn't seem to have any idea of the nuances he had precipitated.

'It's time for dessert. It's Lisa's turn to be in charge.'

Anne helped Lisa clear the plates. Mike and David began discussing an upcoming rugby match. As Lisa carried the masterpiece of the dessert into the room, the phone rang. She hastily put the plate down on the coffee-table. She listened in silence for a minute and then held the phone out.

'Mike? You'd better take this.' Lisa didn't return to the table. She looked worried. 'It's Stephen. His blood pressure's down and he's short of breath. The registrar on says he sounds pretty congested.'

Mike put the phone down within a minute. 'I'll have to go in,' he said calmly. 'Thank goodness I only had the one beer. We're going to have to get an arterial line and Swan-Ganz catheter in. Looks like Stephen's gone into heart failure.'

Lisa stood up. 'I'm coming, too.'

'So am I.' David jumped to his feet. 'He's my patient as well.'

They all looked at Anne. Mike sighed. 'I guess you'll just have to eat all that pavlova by yourself, love.'

'I don't think so.' Anne's face was a picture of dismay. 'Look!'

Sophie held up fistfuls of the flattened pavlova. Her face was entirely covered with whipped cream.

'I'm so sorry, Lisa,' Anne apologised. 'Your beautiful dessert! I'll clean it up.'

'No worries.' Lisa was reaching for her car keys. 'It was David who made the real effort here. I was just pretending.'

David held the door open for Mike and Lisa who

hurried past. She didn't even look at him. The comment rang in his ears. Had she been referring simply to the dinner party?

Or did she mean their entire relationship?

CHAPTER TEN

THEY had all scrubbed up.

If the nurse who had prepared the treatment room had been surprised at the overkill of skilled staff available for the procedure of inserting a Swan-Ganz catheter, she didn't show it. The atmosphere was tense. Everybody wanted Stephen to be a success story, and those who had come to know the teenager in recent weeks were giving no consideration to the hospital's reputation or the media's reaction to an unsuccessful outcome. The determination to see him through this episode of rejection had everything to do with who Stephen was and nothing at all to do with *what* he was.

The nurse quietly finished draping the top half of Stephen's body with sterile green cloths and then handed Mike the syringe of local anaesthetic.

'This'll sting for a second, mate,' Mike told the boy. 'Grit your teeth.'

Stephen was lying with his head tipped slightly down. Lisa checked his oxygen supply and touched the automatic blood-pressure cuff to get an extra reading.

'I took the MG for a run out to Akaroa last weekend,' Lisa told Stephen. 'You should have seen the way she held those hill corners. It was awesome!'

David's eyebrow quirked. It wasn't the car that had been responsible for the breathtaking ride.

'As soon as you're allowed out of this joint for a day or two I'll take you,' Lisa promised. 'We'll really burn some rubber.'

Mike was unclipping the syringe attached to his introducing needle as Lisa talked. He exchanged it for the guide wire David had ready, then swapped the needle for a plastic sheath which slipped into the vein over the top of the wire. He screwed it gently into place.

Lisa was now laughing at something Stephen had said. 'Yeah, right!' She chuckled dubiously. 'And when did you get your driver's licence, then?'

Mike nodded at the radiographer who switched on the fluoroscopy unit. David nodded with satisfaction as Mike skilfully threaded the tip of the catheter through Stephen's heart and into the pulmonary artery.

'Take a deep breath for me, Stephen. Good, now cough!' Mike carefully removed the sheath. 'We're all set to rock and roll,' he announced. 'Stitch that end for me, Dave. Then you won't feel entirely superfluous.'

Lisa kept chatting to Stephen as Mike and the technician set up the pressure transducers and took the initial recordings of the intricate measurements of heart function the catheter was able to provide. Then Lisa was left with the nurse and a new sterile trolley to insert an arterial line in Stephen's arm. Mike and David moved away to launch into a detailed discussion of the heavy drug therapy they needed to balance.

'We'll have to increase the calcium antagonist...'

'Dopamine for the blood pressure...'

'What diuretic do you favour?'

'We'll start the IV steroid treatment, stat...'

'What's the current cyclosporine level?'

Lisa elected to stay in the hospital overnight and gave David her car keys to drive home. Arriving at the town house at 3 a.m. David was confronted by the devastated kitchen. Anne had cleared up the mess Sophie had made with the pavlova. Her note said she was sorry she couldn't do more but Sophie wouldn't settle so she'd had to take her home. She also wished David luck and advised him to find a fresh dishwashing brush.

It took David well over an hour to clean up and he spent most of it wondering whether domesticity was really what he wanted. Being with Lisa, it had a curious effect of throwing him into role reversal situations. Here she was, following the demanding dictates of her chosen profession, and here he was—washing the dishes!

What would happen if their arrangement did become anything more permanent? A series of cooks, house-keepers or even nannies? It wasn't David's idea of an ideal marriage. He might consider himself new age but the prospect of being a househusband was one even Lisa couldn't tempt him into. If they were equal partners, how come he'd cooked the dinner and was now left to clear up as well? Lisa's comment came back to haunt him. He was the one making the real effort. She was just pretending.

The consideration of the potential truth in the state-ment provoked a sense of dissatisfaction that grew over the next few days. Lisa was preoccupied with Stephen and spent another night at the hospital. Even as he be-gan to show definite signs of recovery Lisa spent her time at home reading every textbook and journal article she could lay her hands on that dealt with the manage-ment of organ rejection.

David felt that Stephen's new heart was not the only thing in danger of being rejected. David knew what he wanted. He also knew what Lisa wanted. It seemed like a case of never the twain should meet, and David was left wondering whether he would have to settle for a second-rate compromise if he didn't want to lose Lisa.

He found himself very distracted, searching for some sort of resolution.

'You're very restless.' Lisa looked up from her journal.

'I've got things on my mind.'

'Such as?'

David looked around him. 'Let's buy a house, Lisa.'

'What?' The journal slipped from her fingers. 'Why? What's wrong with this place?'

'Nothing's wrong.' David shrugged helplessly. He couldn't say it didn't feel like a home. Modern, compact and full of textbooks, journals and the overflow of paperwork from the hospital. It felt like a comfortable office extension. 'It's just…yours.'

'Why should that bother you? It's very handy to the hospital. It's not as though we even spend that much time here.'

'Maybe that's the problem.' David drummed his fingers on the arm of the couch. 'Don't you ever feel you'd like more out of life, Lisa? More than just a career?'

Lisa stared at him, her expression disturbingly neutral.

'You told me you get bored, doing the same thing all the time. Don't you get bored, shuttling between here and the hospital? Doesn't it bother you how much time we spend talking to each other about work?'

'Are *you* bored?'

'No… I'm…' David stood up and paced across the room. 'I don't know what I am.' He rubbed wearily at his face. 'I'm tired, I guess. Let's go to bed.' They hadn't made love since the night of Stephen's crisis. Perhaps that was the main cause of his restlessness.

'You go ahead. I just want to finish this article.' Lisa picked up her journal and appeared to be reading again, but David stood still for a moment, staring at her. The vibes weren't great. Perhaps a showdown didn't need to be engineered. Maybe his prevarication was simply postponing the inevitable. If that was the case, he wasn't sure he had any desire to speed the process up.

The showdown was much closer than David had suspected. He was delivering a CT scan result to Lisa on the latest Neuroshield trial patient the next morning when his beeper sounded.

'Mind if I use your phone?'

'Not at all.' Lisa was reading the scan report as she stepped aside. 'Be my guest.'

David cast her a sharp glance but she didn't look up from the report. He hadn't been asleep when she'd finally come to bed last night, but he had pretended to be, wondering whether Lisa would make any attempt to rouse him. Or, hopefully, arouse him. She hadn't. Perhaps that, too, had become an activity repeated endlessly enough to bore her. Her early morning politeness was obviously set to continue. It had the effect of making her appear distant but at the same time antagonistic.

David sighed audibly as he pushed zero to contact the switchboard operator. Perhaps he didn't have the stamina to cope with Lisa long term after all. He knew she coped with stress by becoming bolshy and unapproachable. He also knew he was causing the present level of stress they were experiencing. It wasn't a happy situation.

'We have an outside call for you, Mr James. A collect toll call from Australia. Will you pay the charges?'

'Yeah. Put it through, thanks.' David tried, unsuccessfully, not to let his spirits slide any further.

'Davey? Oh, God!' The sobs on the other end of the

line were clearly audible to Lisa, who looked up questioningly.

'Melanie? What on earth's the matter?' David gave Lisa a dismayed expression and held the phone closer to his ear to try and muffle the other end of the conversation. Lisa turned her back, holding a CT plate up to the light of the window.

'Oh, no!' David groaned. 'Not *again*.' He raised his voice. 'Calm down. Stop *crying*, Melanie.' David waited for the hiccuping to stop and then lowered his voice. 'Just how far overdue are you?' He wished he'd taken this call in his own office. Lisa didn't want to know about his family. If anything was likely to be a complication then Melanie's problems, landing on their doorstep, would surely take first prize.

'Have you had a test? Why not?' David listened in silence for a while. Glancing over his shoulder, he could see the ramrod- like stance of Lisa's back. He had one woman who didn't want what he wanted to offer. Now he had another who wanted more than he wanted to offer. Quite suddenly, David reached the end of his emotional tether. They were an alien species. He'd be better off without any of them.

'For God's sake, Melanie,' he exploded. 'You can't always assume the man is going to take responsibility for birth control. I've told you how I feel about that before. Take the damned test. Ring me later and we'll go from there.' David slammed the phone down with an exasperated growl.

Lisa dropped the CT results envelope on her desk. 'I take it this isn't the first time this has happened?' she enquired calmly.

David was still furious. 'No. And it probably won't be the last. I don't know. *Women!*'

'And you don't want to take any responsibility?'

'Why the hell should I?' David glared at Lisa. 'It's not *my* problem.'

Sean Findlay, bursting into the office as David spoke, stopped in his tracks. 'Oh, sorry. Am I interrupting? I've got a bit of a problem.'

'Don't tell me about it, mate,' David snarled. 'I've got more than enough of my own.'

Lisa failed to put in an appearance at the departmental referral meeting that afternoon. David's relief at Melanie's follow-up phone call evaporated. He waited impatiently to corner Mike when the discussion finally wrapped up.

'Where's Lisa?'

'I'm not sure. She was looking a bit pale. I told her go home if she wasn't well. I haven't seen her since. Hey, did you know we took out Stephen's Swan-Ganz catheter this morning? He's looking great.'

David tried to smile at the good news but his mind was racing. Lisa unwell? Why hadn't she told him? His concern all but obliterated the sound of Mike's voice.

'So we'll do another biopsy on Thursday but we're confident that we've got the rejection under control.' Mike paused. 'You don't look so great yourself, mate. Is there some bug going around?' He peered anxiously into David's face. 'You haven't been using the dish-washing brush to clean the toilet again, have you?'

'I've got to go, Mike. It's urgent.'

Mike clucked sympathetically. 'Hope you get over it soon, mate. It's not like you to get sick.'

David did feel sick. Sick with worry. He tried beep-

ing Lisa to no avail. Going outside, he scanned the staff
car park. It was all too easy to see that the little red
roadster had gone. David walked around the building to
the main entrance and waved tersely to the first taxi in
line at the stand. Within minutes he was flinging open
the door of the town house.

'Lisa? Are you all right?' She wasn't in the kitchen.
The sitting room and bathroom were both empty. David
stopped his frantic search with a painful jolt when he
reached the bedroom door. Lisa was in the bedroom. A
suitcase lay opened on the bed. David stared, stunned.

'What are you doing?'

'Packing.' Lisa didn't look at him but David could
see she had been crying. Her eyes were red, her face
puffy and she sounded like she had a badly blocked
nose.

'God, Lisa!' David took two long strides into the
room and caught her arm. 'What the hell has happened?'

'You. That's what's happened.' Lisa angrily shook
his hand off her arm. 'I was right all along. I should
never have trusted you.'

'Bloody hell, Lisa. What have I *done*?' David
watched as Lisa scooped up the entire contents of her
underwear drawer and dumped them into the suitcase.

'How *could* you, David? The only other time I really
loved someone.' Lisa sniffed loudly. 'He got someone
else pregnant, too, and went off and married her.'

David felt a wave of confusion. 'Lewis?'

'*No!*' Lisa was pulling hangers out of the wardrobe.
She threw the clothes, hangers and all, into a crumpled
heap on top of the underwear. 'The man I was prepared
to…almost did…give up medical school for.' Lisa's
red-rimmed eyes grazed David's. 'I ruined my grades

for a year, thinking I wanted him more than a career. I almost ruined them the next year, getting over it.' Lisa swooped down and grabbed several pairs of shoes, stacking them on one arm. 'It was failing a term paper that cured me. Nobody was going to ruin *my* life.' Lisa jerked to her feet, dropping several shoes. 'That goes for you too, David James. I'm leaving!'

'But this is your house.' David couldn't quite fight off the confusion. It was only now that her words were beginning to sink in. The only other time she had really loved someone. Did that mean she loved *him*?

'Oh, God!' Lisa turned the suitcase upside down, spilling its contents onto the floor. 'Fine. *You* leave, then.'

'I still don't understand, Lisa. Why do either of us have to leave?'

'How can you even ask? Melanie's pregnant and you won't even take any responsibility for it. You're a bastard, David. Or your child will be at any rate.'

'What? Lisa, you *know* Melanie's my sister.'

'Like hell I do.'

'But I told you—that night after Mike and Anne had gone home.'

'I stayed at the hospital remember?'

David groaned. 'And you stayed the next night too. And then I was so worried about what was happening with us that I forgot I hadn't told you after all. Anyway, she rang me. She's not pregnant, after all.'

'Bully for her,' Lisa snapped. 'I don't care any more, David. I've had enough. I *trusted* you. You let me believe Melanie was something special. You could have told me she was your sister a very long time ago.'

'I know.' David's grin was shamefaced. 'I was too

excited about the idea that you might be jealous. I didn't say anything that wasn't true.'

'You implied it,' Lisa snapped. 'And I asked—*specifically*, about her before I asked you to move in. And you *still* didn't say anything.'

'No.' David couldn't deny the accusation. A sensation of impending doom began to close around him. 'I knew how hard it was for you to trust me, Lisa,' he offered quietly. 'I couldn't let myself blow it.'

'Well, you've blown it now, mate.' Lisa stepped angrily over the pile of clothing. 'If you're not going to leave then I am.'

David stepped back and put his arm out to block the door.

'Don't you dare walk out on me.'

'Why not?' Lisa's face radiated pure misery.

'Because you can't.'

'Why *not*?'

David took a deep breath. 'Because I'm going to marry you.'

'Like hell you are.' Lisa's hands were bunched into fists. David wanted nothing more than to take her in his arms, but he couldn't. Not yet.

'Why not?' he echoed gently.

'Because you don't buy books, remember? You've got a whole library to choose from.'

David gave just the ghost of a grin. The aggression meant that Lisa was rattled. She could only be *this* rattled if it was something she cared about passionately. And this was about *him*. 'That's right,' he agreed happily. 'And I've made my choice. The hardest one to read I've ever come across, and I have no intention of ever putting it down.'

Lisa's fists had uncurled but she was still glaring angrily at David. 'I'm still not going to marry you.'

'Why not?' Something loosened in David's chest. A warmth he recognised as having been missing for days now flickered back into life.

'For one thing, you haven't asked me.'

'OK.' David's grin was now half-strength. 'Will you marry me, Lisa?'

'No.'

'Why not?'

'Because you don't want children.'

'Neither do you. You looked appalled when Sophie turned up at our dinner.'

'Only because I knew how much you didn't like kids. You said they weren't on the agenda, remember?'

'I only said that to reassure you. I knew *you* didn't want kids.'

Lisa was staring at his feet. 'Maybe I've changed my mind.

'Maybe I have, too.' David dropped his arm from the doorway. 'I want the place crawling with rugrats. I want a really big house and a smelly dog and carpets full of crisps and pavlova.'

The corner of Lisa's mouth twitched. 'And who's supposed to look after this big house and clean up the carpets and look after the dog and smelly children?'

'Melanie needs a job. It might keep her out of trouble for a while. And the dog can clean up the carpets. Especially the crisps and pavlova.'

'I'm not going to have children and then let someone else bring them up.' Lisa was still trying to sound confrontational but the heat of her argument had been all but extinguished.

'We could collaborate.' David took a step forward so

that he was standing within touching distance of Lisa.
'I think we'd make a great team, Lisa.'

She met his gaze, her face solemn. 'Maybe. But I still
can't marry you.'

'Why? Because you want to stand here and argue the
toss for ever?'

'No.' Lisa's eyes darkened to an impossibly velvet
hue. 'Because I can't marry someone who doesn't love
me.'

'Who said I don't love you?'

'You've never said you did.'

They stared at each other in the sudden silence that
fell. In her stockinged feet Lisa had to look up to meet
David's gaze. Her eyes told him everything he needed
to know. Her feelings were written plainly over every
adored feature. David's mouth curled in a gentle smile
and Lisa's lips trembled as they mimicked the movement.

'Hey, Lisa?'

'What?'

'I love you.' David caught hold of both her hands.
'You drive me crazy and I can't possibly live without
you.'

'Good.'

'Is that it? I tell you I love you and that you drive
me crazy and all you can say is ''good''? Aren't you
even going to argue about it?'

'Not this time.' Lisa reached up to touch David's
cheek softly. 'I meant it's good that you can't possibly
live without me.' Her fingers traced the outline of his
lips. 'I love you, too, David. You're not going to get
the chance to live without me.'

'Does this mean we actually agree with each other?

We can share our careers and still have the kids...and the house...and the dog...and the pavlova?'

'I'll *make* the pavlova,' Lisa promised. 'Even if it turns out as flat as my omelettes. But, David?'

'Mmm?' His lips were hovering close enough to feel the movement of her words. He thought he didn't need to hear anything else Lisa might want to say just then but her lips were moving again and David knew he had been wrong.

'Do you think we could get married first?'

MILLS & BOON®

Makes
any time
special

Enjoy a romantic novel from
Mills & Boon®

Presents...™ *Enchanted*™ TEMPTATION.

Historical Romance™ ⊣*MEDICAL*
ROMANCE

MILLS & BOON®

MEDICAL ROMANCE™

GOOD HUSBAND MATERIAL by Sheila Danton

Rebecca Groom soon realises how attractive she finds the senior partner, Dr Marc Johnson. But the surgery intends to expand, using an old house that holds dear memories for Rebecca…

ALWAYS MY VALENTINE by Leah Martyn

Charge Nurse Geena Wilde liked Dr Jack O'Neal very much, but it wasn't until Valentine's Day that Geena received a gorgeous bunch of red roses from Jack, and an invitation to the Valentine Ball! That was a *very* good beginning…

COURTING DR CADE by Josie Metcalfe

Damon and Katherine were instant friends. Now Katherine's grandmother will lose her beloved home unless Katherine is married by Leap Year's day! But a simple marriage of convenience turns into something far more complicated!

A FAMILY CONCERN by Margaret O'Neill

For Gemma Fellows and her six-year-old daughter, Daisy, the cottage is a godsend. It's a new start—and as far as Dr Sam Mallory is concerned, Gemma and Daisy are perfect for him…

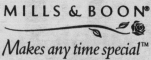

4 FREE
books and a surprise gift!

We would like to take this opportunity to thank you for reading this Mills & Boon® book by offering you the chance to take FOUR more specially selected titles from the Medical Romance™ series absolutely FREE! We're also making this offer to introduce you to the benefits of the Reader Service™—

- ★ FREE home delivery
- ★ FREE gifts and competitions
- ★ FREE monthly Newsletter
- ★ Exclusive Reader Service discounts
- ★ Books available before they're in the shops

Accepting these FREE books and gift places you under no obligation to buy, you may cancel at any time, even after receiving your free shipment. Simply complete your details below and return the entire page to the address below. *You don't even need a stamp!*

YES! Please send me 4 free Medical Romance books and a surprise gift. I understand that unless you hear from me, I will receive 6 superb new titles every month for just £2.40 each, postage and packing free. I am under no obligation to purchase any books and may cancel my subscription at any time. The free books and gift will be mine to keep in any case.

M0EA

Ms/Mrs/Miss/Mr ....Initials.................../.......
BLOCK CAPITALS PLEASE

Surname ....

Address ....

....

....Postcode................................

Send this whole page to:
UK: FREEPOST CN81, Croydon, CR9 3WZ
EIRE: PO Box 4546, Kilcock, County Kildare (stamp required)